I0682607

Dead Men's Shoes

By G. H. Teed

First published in **Union Jack** magazine
20 Nov. 1912, No. 477 Series 2.

Stillwoods Edition, 2019

Stillwoods.Blogspot.Ca

Catalogue Information:
Title: Dead Men's Shoes
Author: G. H. Teed
First published in Union Jack magazine 20 Nov. 1912, No. 477 Series 2.
This Edition: Stillwoods, 2019. (Doug Frizzle)
ISBN Canada: 978-1-988304-95-3
Blog: Stillwoods.Blogspot.Ca
Author Blog: http://ghteed.blogspot.com/
Storefront: http://www.lulu.com/spotlight/lulubook22

Copyright © Doug Frizzle and/or Stillwoods Publishing, 2019.

Keywords: Sexton Blake, British fictional detective.

The Skipper desires to draw his readers' attention to the fact that "DEAD MEN'S SHOES" has been written expressly for this issue of the UNION JACK.

Chief Characters in this Story.

Sexton Blake	The Great British Detective.
Tinker	His Clever Young Assistant.
Pedro	Blake's World-famed Bloodhound.

and
William Saunders   alias Jim Ford and Jim Carson.
Harris   Butler to Mr. Alliston.
James   Groom at Alliston Hall,
John Alliston, alias William Torrence…... Heir to Alliston Hall.

John Alliston, alias William Torrence loses his fortune in a gamble to double his fortunes. At the same time he is watched and later attacked, losing everything—even his real identity. Then he is convicted of killing one of his gambling company.

Eventually he earns his freedom, but his identity in England is covered by another, and his Father is murdered.

Blake takes the solution of this murderer under task from Jack Alliston, grandson and heir apparent to Alliston Hall.

Stillwoods Editions are a poor complement to some great stories and authors. Doug Frizzle is 'Stillwoods'; in retirement I needed something to do on 'foul weather' days.

First I found the author, A. Hyatt Verrill, from New Haven, Conn. He had been prolific and popular in his time but was forgotten even to Wikipedia. His books were difficult to locate—they were acquired from used book dealers as far away as Australia and South Africa. They were such great reading I began to republish them. I started with an autobiography of the author, unpublished, that I located at University of British Columbia—that Archive had no idea how they acquired it!

So I entered the publishing business. I am using Lulu.Com; it is a print on demand publisher so the costs are quite manageable. I spent 15 years on Verrill!

Then I found 'Luke Allan', a Canadian, namely, Lacey Amy, who wrote stories while he travelled the world, but they were mostly about 'Blue Pete' an American Half-breed who evades his enemies by going to Canada; Medicine Hat, Alberta, to be exact, and is befriended by a Mountie. Again these books were scarce, and no one knew this author was a Canadian. There are Stillwoods Editions of all of his 54 novels—two were published anonymously!

Lately, I've discovered New Brunswick's G. H. Teed, 1886-1938—prolific and forgotten. The vast majority of his 400+ novels were published anonymously and as 'pulp' novels. They were available weekly on England's newsstands and were very popular but as they were made of inferior paper, they deteriorated quickly. But over the years, English collectors speculated and researched these works, discovering a series of authors, and G. H. Teed was one of the greatest!

Teed's works were mystery and suspense—detective novels featuring 'Sexton Blake' or 'Nelson Lee' as cerebral sleuths with great physical training. As this 'About Stillwoods' is being created, one collector of Sexton Blake has provided me with some 200 scans of Teed novels. At this time I have re-published about 65 of his works as either blog posts, or, the longer stories as Lulu imprints.

So that is the story on Stillwoods and myself, there are a few other authors and works I have added along in my journeys.

The quality of Stillwoods Editions is perhaps not great. I have no training in any of this digitizing and publishing business. I do not stop to make perfect products. I would rather have ten ones, than one ten!

I hope you enjoy these authors—their works are nearly a hundred years old!

Thanks to the author and collector, Mark Hodder, many of the Sexton Blake stories by G. H. Teed stories have been made available to Stillwoods Publisher. Many thanks to Mark!!!

Disclaimer: Each work may contain language and racial terms that are not appropriate to today. I apologize for them; I know that the author was using his voice to excite an adventurous English audience. Most every work has characters of redeeming ethnicity within.

I hope you enjoy and share these stories; I have.

Doug Frizzle

frizzle@hfx.eastlink.ca

About G. H. Teed

There are discrepancies in the reports on the history of G. H. Teed. This narrative is mine and may be more or less accurate.

George Heber Teed was born 1886 near Saint Stephen, New Brunswick, Canada. His father was a landowner and entrepreneur. He was educated in New Brunswick and then was sent to McGill University, where he probably graduated about 1907.

He had an itch for travel and for the Caribbean; once the travel bug got him he travelled far. He worked in Costa Rica and Australia before he travelled to England and began to write detective thrillers.

He was not great with money, he was very social and spent much time in taverns. Reports are that he was often in debt even though he was a prolific writer in popular magazines.

He took some time off in war service in the Great War.

He spent considerable time in France.

He also took a few years off around 1921, again getting the travel bug. These travels were around the world. These travels added authenticity to his stories, and his stories always had excellent plots and characters.

He died in 1938. Some of his works are listed as by G. Hamilton Teed—apparently he did not like Heber, so he adopted Hamilton as a familiar name.

Perhaps the best description of the man and his works is contained in the book '**Forgotten Authors Volume 3**' by Steve Holland.

G. H. Teed books available at:

http://www.lulu.com/spotlight/lulubook22

Bottom of Suez
Crooks' Vendetta
Voodoo Island
Five in Fear
The Grey Ghost
The Case of the Duplicate Key
The Temple of Many Visions
Gangland's Decree
The Clue of the Four Wigs
The Mystery of the Film City
The Black Abbot
Murder Ship
Spies Ltd.
A Mystery of the Big Woods
The Mystery of the Kidnapped Killer
The Secret of the Swamp
The Case of the Pink Macaw
The Terror of Gold-digger Creek
The Case of the Mummified Hand
Pearls of Doom
The Victim of the Gang
The Case of the Courtlandt Jewels
Nelson Lee and the Lhassa Red Menace
The Riddle of the Russian Gold
Voodoo Vengeance
Hounded Down
Bribery and Corruption
The Sacred Sphere
The Tiger of Canton
The Crook of Marsden Manor
The Affair of the Six Ikons
The Secret of the Coconut Groves
The Case of the Disguised Apache

Under the Eagle's Wing
The Rogues' Republic
The Mitcham Murder Mystery
The Brotherhood of the Yellow Beetle
When Greek Meets Greek
Bootleg Island
The Broken Span
The Lumber Looters
The Green Rose
Beyond the Reach of the Law
Dead Men's Shoes

See http://ghteed.blogspot.com/
For some of G. H. Teed's shorter works and articles about this
Canadian author.

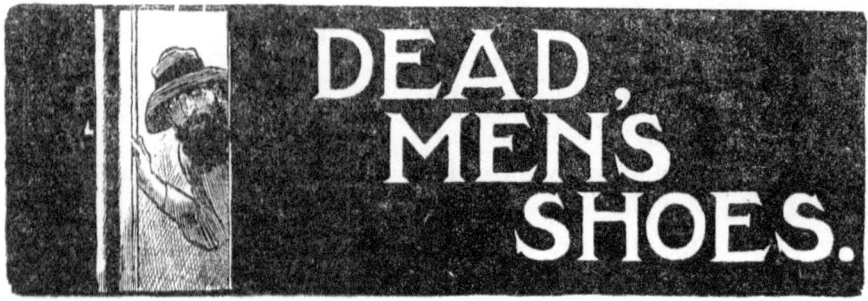

"THE Jack wins and the seven loses; the four wins and the three loses; the two wins and the ace loses."

The voice of the faro dealer, who sat at one end of the table, went on monotonously as he pulled the cards from the dealing-box and turned them face up on the table.

At the other end sat the case-keeper, while between them was the solitary player, placing his bets as he lost, and collecting his very occasional winnings as they turned up.

The room was lit by a smoky lamp. Behind the player ranged a rude bar, typical of the Nevada mining camp in the earlier days of the Tonopah rush, over which lounged a tough-looking bar-keeper, imbibing some of his own poison, many bottles of which decorated the shelves behind him. He was watching the game with a languid interest. On a bench in the corner lay a man, the abandon of whose attitude indicated a drunken stupor.

It was past two in the morning, and the silence was only broken by the droning of the dealer's voice and the clink of the player's money.

The player was a big man, as even his slouching position at the table showed. He was young, almost a boy, with a frank, engaging countenance, and pleasant eyes which were clouded at the moment with the tense look of the gambler.

Luck had been dead against him all the evening, and he had been doubling and re-doubling his stakes in the hope of a turn. But that it was past two in the morning, and the dealer still sat at the table, testified to the fact that he was a profitable customer.

Earlier in the evening the place had been crowded with miners, but they had all departed with the exception of the player and the drunken individual in the corner.

"Your luck's a bit off to-night, Torrence," remarked the dealer, as he tore the wrapper off a fresh pack of cards. "If I were you I'd cut it out for to-night."

"Go ahead with the dealing, and don't waste so much time? Keep your voice for those that need it!" growled the man called Torrence, in reply.

"All right, old man; keep your shirt on! It's your funeral, not mine," grinned the dealer. "Place your bets! The six wins and five loses; the seven wins and the four loses; the three wins and the ace loses." And so the game went on.

Pushing his chair back from the table with an oath, the player rose to his feet.

"Potter come and irrigate." he remarked. "You've got me cleaned out to-night all right."

"I never saw such a run in my life," said the case-keeper, joining them at the bar. "If a man had played the cards to lose what you played to win, he'd have broke the bank."

"Well, come on, bur-keep, fill them up! I suppose it's five minutes since you had one yourself, and since you are not a camel, you had better join us," Torrence sarcastically remarked.

"Waal," drawled the bar-keep, "I reckon it would make even a camel thirsty to watch you burning holes in the table. How about our weary friend in the corner? Is he joining?"

"I guess not," grinned the dealer. "His last intelligent state was over two hours ago, when he was entertaining himself with a very careful recital of Paul Revere's Ride. Well, here's better luck next time!" he remarked, tossing down his drink. "If you want a hundred to stake you, Torrence, you're welcome to it." he added.

"No, thanks!" replied Torrence. "I think I've had about enough. I'd be a bit suspicious of the game if it was anybody dealing but you, Jerry. By the way, Haynes," he asked, turning to the case-keeper, "what cards are left in the dealer's box?"

"There is a ten and a seven," replied the man, looking at his record.

"How much will you stake against that on a last turn of the cards, Jerry?" asked Torrence, pulling a folded paper from his pocket and passing it to the dealer.

"Where did you get this?" inquired the dealer, looking at him quickly. "And is there much there?" he added.

"I found it myself, and made that plan out. It's simply full of the stuff, but needs machinery put in to crush the quartz, and that's why I was trying to get a turn on the table to-night. It's all straight. You may take my word for that. There's a million in that mine," he added.

"I'll tell you what I'll do," replied the dealer. "You pick on the last turn of the cards, and I'll stake you twenty-five thousand dollars against this plan."

"Done!" snapped Torrence, banging the bar with his fist. "Give us another drink, Camel, for luck!" he shouted.

As the quartet lifted their glasses, none of them saw the man in the corner quietly shift his position so that he might have a better view of the table.

Resuming their positions, Torrence leaned his head on his left hand, and it might have been seen that the little finger was missing. He stared at the dealer's box, as though he would perhaps find some information in its shining silver sides as to which would be the winning card.

"Only the ten and the seven left," he muttered, "and that cursed seven has beaten me all the evening! I've played it steadily to win, and it's lost all the time. The chances are if I play it this time to lose, the hanged thing will win. I'll play it again to win."

"Well, Torrence, which is it?" asked the dealer.

"Go ahead! I'll pick the seven again to win!"

The atmosphere of the room was tense. The bar-keeper leaned, fascinated, over his bar, and the case-keeper's fingers shook nervously as he lit a cigarette, while even the dealer, accustomed as he was to playing for fortunes in a single throw, felt the excitement of the moment. Apparently the coolest of the lot was Torrence, who was risking all he had in the world on that one turn of the cards. But none of them noticed the interest displayed by the man in the corner, whom they all thought was in a drunken sleep.

"You decide on the seven to win, do you?" asked the dealer, wetting his finger.

"Yes. For Heaven's sake turn it up, and let's get it over!"

"The ten wins and the seven loses!" called the dealer, endeavouring to keep his voice steady.

"That finishes it!" ejaculated Torrence, pushing over the plan to him. "I thought that seven would beat me again. I could take you and your table and dump you down the Mogul Mine!" he growled, getting to his feet. "Goodnight!" he muttered, stumbling to the door and banging it after him.

"Have a drink before you go?" called the dealer. But Torrance did not hear him. "Well, it's been a good evening," he continued. "A clean ten thousand in cash from Torrence, besides this plan of his; and it's worth a hundred thousand dollars if it's worth a cent. You'd better wake up old sleepy head, and toss him out," he added, turning to the bar-keeper.

And as he spoke, the man in the corner gave a resounding snore.

"All right," answered the bar-keeper, pouring out a glass of whisky as he spoke. "I'll just give old Rip Van Winkle this to keep him awake till he gets home."

He walked over to the recumbent figure in the corner, and shook him violently.

"Come on, my pretty child, and smell the beautiful flowers!" he yelled in his ear, holding the whisky under his nose.

The man roused himself heavily, and as he brought his arm down from his head he hit the tumbler in the barkeeper's hand, and it fell to the floor with a crash.

"Come on, Jumbo! You've spilled the only drink you'll get here to-night. Wake up!" And the bar-keeper jerked him to his feet, where he stood blinking in the light, as though still under the influence of the liquor.

Dragged to the door and assisted through it by the barkeeper's foot, he lurched up the embryo street of the mining camp until he had disappeared from the path of light which shone through the window of the saloon.

Inside the saloon, the faro dealer and his assistant had gathered up their money and their belongings, and the bar-keeper had collected his cash. Turning out the light, they emerged from the saloon, and stood chatting for a moment. The dealer bade the others good-night, and, turning, struck off for his camp, while the bar-keeper and the assistant strolled off in the opposite direction.

As the dealer swung off up the trail towards his own cavern, he was probably engrossed calculating his profits of the night, for he did not see a dark figure which stealthily followed him, gradually drawing nearer and nearer as they approached the deep shaft of the mine.

As he turned the corner of the pile of tailings, he paused to light a cigarette. That match was the last he ever struck! The man following had crept closer and closer, and as the dealer lifted the match to his cigarette, he brought down the butt end of a Colt's revolver with crushing force on the back of his head.

The dealer dropped like a shot. His assailant leaned over, and, opening his coat, rifled the pockets, transferring the contents to his own. Picking up the senseless form of his victim, he dragged it to the mouth of the mine shaft, and pushed it over. He stood listening as the body fell, but the sound of its arrival at the bottom did not reach him in that thousand-foot shaft.

He turned and kicked some of the loose tailings over the marks of his footprints, and, pulling a flask from his pocket, coolly took a long drink. He slipped the flask back in his pocket and stole up the trail.

•   •   •   •

Torrence sat before an almost dead fire in his rough hut. His elbows rested on his knees, and his chin in the palms of his hands.

For hours he sat there, motionless, his lips moving silently at times. His eyes were hard, and his jaw squared, as he raised his hand and spoke.

"The last time—I swear it! Not another card will I touch again! Everything gone! Nothing left! Not even my name!"

And he laughed harshly.

"To think that I, John Alliston, should come to this. Thank Heaven, I have at least achieved my ruin under the assumed name of Torrence! I should have destroyed my private papers long ago. To-morrow I will do so, and again change my name. I'll have to go back over the mountains, and try my luck at finding another claim. What a fool I've been!"

And he groaned.

"That claim I lost to-night would have rivalled the Mogul. But never again, I swear it!"

With which final resolve he rose, and, stumbling to the cot in the corner, threw himself down fully dressed. Five minutes later he was in a heavy sleep.

He could have been a much lighter sleeper and still not heard the silent figure which noiselessly opened the door, and crept stealthily across the room. Even the new-comer's hand, feeling cautiously in the pockets of the sleeping man's coat, did not waken him; and a smile of triumph told of the intruder's success as he pulled some papers from Torrence's pocket, and glanced hurriedly at them.

A moment later he had glided to the door, and was soon lost in the mist and darkness.

II.   The Arrest of Torrence—The Trial—Sentenced to Life Imprisonment.

TORRENCE was awakened by the sound of many voices and the trampling of heavy feet. He sat up, and rubbed his eyes, staring stupidly as angry words broke on his ears.

"There he is; lynch him!" cried several voices. And the amazed Torrence dropped his hand to his hip. "What do you mean? What is the matter?" he asked, suddenly wide awake.

"Matter!" they cried. "You ask what the matter is? Is it such a small thing to toss a man down the Mogul Shaft?"

"Toss a man—" began Torrence, but broke off, as a big man pushed aside the crowd of rough miners, and addred him.

"See here, Torrence," he said, "as a private citizen. I respect you; but as sheriff I've got to do my duty, so throw me your gun!"

Torrence complied with the request, and waited for more, "I've got to arrest you," continued the sheriff, as he thrust the revolver in his pocket, "for the murder of Jerry Watson, the faro dealer!"

"What!" gasped Torrence. "I don't understand!"

"He can bluff all right!" growled a miner in the rear, but closed up as Torrence glanced quickly at him.

"Listen, sheriff!" said Torrence. "This is all Greek to me. Do I understand that Jerry Watson has been murdered?"

"Yes,"

"Where?"

"He was thrown down the Mogul Shaft."

And the sheriff shrugged his shoulders, for he believed Torrence to be bluffing.

"But why am I accused?" asked Torrence, bewildered.

"You were playing faro in the Red Dog last night, weren't you?" inquired the sheriff.

"Yes; but—"

"You lost a plan of some claim which you had found somewhere, didn't you?"

"Yes; I found gold beyond the northern range last week."

"Well, the case-keeper and the bar-keeper both say that when you got up from the table you were sore at losing, and said you could throw Jerry and his table down the Mogul Shaft. Jerry was found dead at the bottom of that shaft this morning."

6

"But there was another man in the saloon also!" protested Torrence.

"Only Jim Carson," replied the sheriff. "He was drunk when he left. I've already been at his shack, and searched him, He was still in a drunken sleep, and we found nothing. It would have been impossible for him to do it. No, Torrence, it's no good bluffing! You'll have to come with me, but I'm going to search you first."

"I've only got some private papers in my coat—" began Torrence as he thrust his hand into the inside pocket; but his jaw dropped as it came back empty. "I've been robbed!" he gasped. "There's some devilish trick, sheriff!"

"I guess that's no good, Torrence!" grinned the sheriff, "I'm not a boy to be fooled so easy!"

A close search by the sheriff and the miners failed to reveal anything.

"He's hidden them!" growled several.

But though they tore up the boards in the floor, and looked in every possible place, they found nothing.

The sheriff finally gave it up, and led the puzzled Torrence away.

Seeing his word was laughed at, Torrence said nothing more about the papers; but he racked his brains to clear the mystery of their sudden disappearance. He knew they had been there when he lay down, but no explanation came to his bewildered mind.

· · · · ·

The little court-room was packed with interested spectators. The prisoner, William Torrence, was fairly well known, but the deceased faro dealer, Gerald Watson, was known far and wide, and the finding of his dead body at the bottom of the Mogul Shaft had resulted with the arrest and charging with murder of Torrence.

Intense interest centred round the trial, and at the end of the argument and cross-examination it seemed a foregone conclusion that the prisoner would be convicted.

He had consistently denied all knowledge of the affair, but the circumstances as outlined by the prosecuting counsel pointed strongly to the prisoner's guilt, and as the judge started to deliver his address to the jury, eager suspense sat on the faces of the spectators:

"Gentlemen of the jury, you have heard how the prisoner at the Bar, William Torrence, was gambling in the Red Dog saloon. You have heard the sworn evidence of the barkeeper at the saloon, and of the assistant of the deceased, that the prisoner said before leaving. He could toss the deceased and his table to the bottom of the Mogul Shaft. James Carson, the other occupant of the saloon, is of no use as a witness, for he was not in the condition to hear anything that was said. You have heard how the bar-keeper and the assistant went home together, while the deceased went off in the opposite direction alone. You have heard how the deceased faro dealer, Gerald Watson, was found dead the next morning at the bottom of the Mogul Shaft. For the defence you have heard an uncorroborated denial, but the character of the accused was of the highest until the occurrence of this unfortunate affair. I charge you to consider the evidence you have heard, and, without fear or favour, decide in your minds whether the prisoner is innocent or guilty. You will now retire!"

Twenty minutes later the jury filed in and took their places. The judge stood up.

"Gentlemen of the jury, do you find the prisoner guilty or not guilty?"

"Guilty!"

"Stand up, William Torrence! You have been judged guilty of a most cowardly crime by a jury of your fellow-men. I have no remarks to make on the subject, but it is within my province to mitigate your sentence. In view of the fact that no incriminating evidence has been produced other than the remark you made in the Red Dog saloon, and that you have been convicted on circumstantial evidence only, I am going to exercise my privilege. Instead of sentencing you to death, I sentence you to the State Prison for the rest of your natural life!"

The prisoner at the Bar turned deathly white at the sentence, but did not falter. As he was led away by the warders, he saw at the back of the court-room a man whose features were vaguely familiar, with a sardonic smile on his face.

III.   Ten Years Later — The Prison Fire —Torrence Leads the Rescue—Pardoned:

THE great State Prison lay wrapped in darkness. Its unyielding outlines stretched as a darker blotch against the darker sky. The encircling, forbidding walls prevented any light from showing, but, inside there was an occasional gleam. The steady pacing of the guards in the corridors broke the silence within the walls, accompanied by the restless murmur of a new arrival or the tortured raving of a prison-sick mind.

Convict No. 8072 lay sleepless on his hard bed. Ten years of prison life had aged him, and the continual thought of injustice had embittered him. No light of hope shone to him through the grey walls, and he had abandoned himself, in despair, to the living death.

"Life," he whispered to himself—"a life sentence for nothing! I wonder how many are, like myself, living the prison life of shadowed hopes, innocent of wrong-doing? Surely it is enough to make a man ask why—why—why?" He went on softly to himself: "What can be the reason of Fate's ruling which permits such a thing—the guiltless to spend a life of misery, while the guilty fatten on the results?" He sighed heavily as these thoughts passed through his mind, for as time went on they increased in intensity.

He was gradually sinking into a fitful sleep, when a bell crashed out and brought him to his feet in the darkness, Hurrying footsteps soon followed.

"Someone escaped," he muttered, as he strained his ears, listening. "No; it's not the escape-bell, it's inside."

But the smell of invading smoke told him the truth, and he hastily put on his clothes.

"Might get a chance in the excitement," he thought.

Doors were being rapidly thrown open, and the startled inmates dragged forth, to be huddled with others under the menacing guns of the massed guards.

"Here, get a gait on!" said one, throwing open No. 8072's cell door. "No monkey-tricks, either, or you'll get daylight let into you pretty quick! The show's on fire!" he added, as No. 8072 started to leave the cell.

As the convict got outside, his eyes were met with a pitiable sight. Men who had been strong mentally and physically when they entered those walls, had lost every shred of strength by their hopeless existence, and stood cowering before the guards. A few others stood indifferent, not caring what happened, while here and there an alert eye betokened the man who intended making a break for freedom in the excitement of the moment.

No. 8072 joined the others, and the remaining cells soon emptied their occupants.

The smoke was getting intense, and the guards shifted uneasily as they waited for the last lot of prisoners to arrive.

That crowd of prisoners in their present mental state could easily get out of hand. One small thing might start a panic, and the guns of the guards would be of little avail if a concerted rush took place.

"Get into line, and march!" called the sergeant, as be detailed five men to lead them. "The first man who moves out of that line will be shot instantly!" he continued. "The fire is bad, but we're going to get through it all right, so don't lose your heads. Remember, now, the first man who disobeys will be dropped in his tracks. Forward!" And the remarkable procession moved along the corridor.

As they came into the main passage they could see the flames ahead of them. The chapel was a raging mass, and it was spreading quickly, its hungry tongues seizing on anything available. The prison was out of date, and the new one should have been put up long before. The present structure had a wood interior, and it was this which the flames were consuming.

When the convicts saw the flames in front of them, and escape seemed hopeless, it created just the spark necessary to start the other flame of panic, and before the guards could prevent them, the prisoners had turned and dashed madly back the way they had come. Shooting was useless, and the guards were greatly outnumbered. They turned and followed the panic-stricken prisoners, whom they found cowering at the other end of the passage. Kicks, curses, and blows were of little avail; the flames were spreading rapidly, and a move must be made soon. It was then that No. 8072 came to the front and took the leadership. The guards, in the strain of the moment, forgot his uniform. They heard only his commanding voice, which they unhesitatingly obeyed. His leadership was unquestioned, and he soon had a semblance of order restored.

Telling the guards off in pairs, he had each pair seize a struggling prisoner. Carrying their burden to the upper gallery and through the passage leading to the corner lookout room, they thrust him forth, and the waiting firemen outside took him down. As each pair of guards deposited his burden, they returned for another and another, until the number of helpless convicts had decreased. Some of them walked the journey, but several, who had refused to go, still remained. The flames were eating their way nearer and nearer to the corridor, and it would soon be impossible to pass up to the gallery.

As the guards felt the hot breath of the fire, they, too, lost their nerve and refused to brave it again.

No. 8072, seizing one of the rifles which had been thrown down by them, levelled it, and threatened to shoot the first guard who refused, forcing them, in this manner, to proceed. Two more trips were made—the last one on the run—and only one man remained. It was madness to brave the fire again. It looked hopeless. There was only one chance in a thousand of getting through and back; but No. 8072 took that chance. Dashing through, he seized the whimpering man and fought his way back, through the licking tongues of flame and smoke, dropping exhausted on the floor of the look-out-room. But he had rescued the man, and to him belonged the credit of the saving of more than seventy lives.

The guards soon recovered their authoritative manner on reaching the ground, and half an hour later No. 8072 and his fellow-convicts were marched, under guard, to temporary quarters.

　　•　　　•　　　•　　　•　　　•

"You're to come with me!"

It was a prison guard who spoke, in a sharp tone to No. 8072, who sat in his temporary cell.

The guards had never quite forgiven him for his assumption of authority during the panic, and the convict suffered accordingly.

He rose without question and followed the guard, who conducted him through the building and down the stairs to an office on the ground-floor.

Knocking at a door, the guard stood aside, and No. 8072 entered, to find himself in the presence of the governor of the prison, who sat at a desk facing him.

"You are No. 8072?" he inquired, as the prisoner entered.

"Yes, sir."

"Let me see," continued the governor, consulting a paper before him. "Your name is Torrence?"

"Yes, sir."

"Well, Torrence, it has come to my ears regarding your conduct during the fire at the prison. I investigated the reports and found them to be true. I made representations on the matter to the State Governor, and, in view of your bravery, and also considering the fact that you were committed to prison on circumstantial evidence, I am pleased to tell you that he has granted you a free pardon, without any conditions attached thereto."

No. 8072 felt everything swimming before him. A pardon! He could hardly believe his ears. It must be a mad joke! He struggled to speak, but his emotion was too great for him. Finally, he gasped.

"Is it true?"

"Yes, Torrence, it is true," and the governor smiled kindly. "Come, man, pull yourself together and prepare yourself to leave! I have had an outfit purchased for you, and have also to present you with a cheque, with the thanks of the State. It will give you a start in life again, and I trust you will use it well."

Torrence mechanically took the slip of paper which the governor held out, and shaking the hand which was also presented to him, he mumbled his thanks and stumbled from the room, scarcely able to grasp the fact that he was free.

Free! What music that word had in it! How he rolled it over his tongue and dinned it at himself repeatedly. Free— free—free! Free to go back to England! Free to find the man who had sent him to prison, as he thought, for life! Free to hold his head up as other men!

He hastened back to his cell and donned the clothes which had been placed there in his absence. He then returned to the prison office, and thanking the governor in a more collected manner, he passed out; and as the prison door clanged behind him, he went forth into the new life.

The End of the Prologue.

THE STORY.

THE MAN IN THE CORNER.

JERRY WATSON'S PERIL.

INSPECTOR THOMAS ARRIVES.

TINKER TRAPPED IN THE BOWERY

THE FIRST CHAPTER.   Charles Alliston, the Wealthy Mill-Owner —He Tells His Grandson Jack the Story of His Life—The Butler Overhears.

"DID you ring, sir?"

"Yes. Has Master Jack finished packing, Harris?"

"I'm not sure, sir; but I'll go and see."

"Tell him, when he has finished, I wish to speak to him."

"Very good, sir!" And the man withdrew.

Mr. Charles Alliston leaned back and stared at the ceiling.

His elbows were supported on the arms of the chair which he occupied, in front of a magnificent mahogany desk, and his fingertips were pressed together. His whole attitude denoted deep thought, and such, indeed, was the case.

The room in which he sat was a luxuriously-furnished library. The walls were lined with shelves, in which reposed hundreds of rare editions, for Charles Alliston was an enthusiastic collector. On the tops of the cases and over the large, open fireplace were many strange curios from all parts of the world and of all ages of man. The carpet was of the kind into which one's feet sank with a delightful sensation, and a couple of valuable rugs were thrown carelessly on it—one before the desk and the other before the fireplace. Several massive mahogany chairs and a few choice engravings completed the furnishings. A log fire burning in the large fireplace threw a softening light on the dignified outlines of the room.

Charles Alliston was the sole owner of the large steelworks in the village which bore his name. His magnificent home lay about two miles from it, the extensive grounds running to the village limits. He was a man well past middle age, but he often remarked he felt thirty, and, indeed, a look at his stalwart figure, straight as a ramrod, as he walked about his works each day, would have impressed one of the truth of his words. His eyes were of a clear blue, and lit up his face pleasantly when he smiled; but of late years, that had been seldom. His scanty hair was white, and a pointed white beard and moustache completed the dignified and pleasant impression that one received of him. As he sat at his desk that chill late summer's day, he seemed to harmonise completely with the solid and impressive lines of the room.

He sighed deeply, and his hands parted. One mechanically lifting a silver cigar-case, and the other feeling unconsciously for a match.

14

Lighting a cigar, whose delicate aroma showed an intelligent desire for good tobacco and the means to gratify it, he rose and began placing slowly up and down the room, his feet making no sound as they sank into the thick carpet. His eyes held a look of brooding sadness, and an occasional involuntary sigh escaped him.

As a knock came at the door, he halted at the desk. The heavy, dark curtains covering it parted, and a boy entered. He was tall, and good to look upon, and his eyes were of the same deep blue as those of the man at the desk. His features showed a great likeness to those of the man, and his figure gave promise of developing into a similar stalwart straightness. It was obvious a close blood relationship existed between them, and the boy's words as he entered proved it to be so.

"Harris tells me you wish to speak with me, grandfather."

"Yes, Jack, I do," replied the man, his eyes softening as he looked at the boy. "Draw up a chair, my boy," he added, resuming his own.

The boy did as he was bid, and waited for the man to begin. A log fell down in the fireplace, and the mounting flame threw a flickering light over the man's face, increasing the look of sadness in the eyes.

Neither the man nor the boy heard the suppressed breathing of a stealthy figure, which, softly opened the door and stood listening, protected by the heavy curtains. It would have been difficult to recognise in the sinister cunning portrayed on the listening man the usual obsequious expression of Harris.

"Have you finished your packing, Jack?" asked Mr. Alliston as he puffed slowly, at his cigar.

"Yes, sir, quite; it is all ready for James to take to the station, and I have nothing to do now before I go."

"Very well, I will ring presently, and send orders to have it taken. You have over an hour yet," he continued, pulling out his watch and glancing at it, "and I wish to have a talk with you."

"All right, grandfather; but I can't think of anything I've done," and he wrinkled his brows in anxious perplexity.

"It is nothing like that, Jack," replied the man, smiling as he spoke, but quickly growing grave again.

"What is it, grandfather? You look worried. I'm sorry, sir. I thought you wanted to speak to me about something I had done," and he looked with affectionate anxiety at the man.

"You will be sixteen next month, Jack, and before you return to school to-day, I have decided to tell you the true facts of your life," replied Mr. Alliston, after a short sigh.

"I knew there was something about my life which you had reserved from me, and I knew it made you sad at times, sir."

"You are right, my boy; and if you will give me your attention I will tell you the facts," and he sighed deeply. "Your father," he continued presently, "was my only son, I brought him up to be my heir and successor in the mills. He was a strong-willed boy, and developed into a stronger-willed man; but we were very happy here. He had been home from school for about a year when his mother died," and the man's eyes grew moist at the memory. "After her death," he went on, "Jack—his name was the same as yours— started remaining away in the evenings. I thought nothing of it until he came to me one day at the office and said he had married the daughter of one of my employees. I flew into a rage, and drove him from me, telling him never to set foot in the door again. He took me at my word, and never did. I heard that he worked at anything he could get for about a year until your birth, which was also the occasion of your mother's death. He placed you in the care of his wife's parents, and left for abroad, saying he would write. Not a word has been received from him since that day, although I have advertised all over the world and in several different languages. One day at the mills, your mother's father, who still worked for me, saved my life. That incident brought us more in touch with each other, and I finally persuaded them to let me take you. You were about four years old at the time, and have been with me ever since."

Mr. Alliston paused to relight his cigar, and the boy's unsteady breathing showed his suppressed emotion.

"I am satisfied," said Mr. Alliston, continuing his narrative, "that something must have prevented your father from writing, because he was not the type of man to break his word. I feel confident he will yet return, and as you are now old enough to realise what it means, I want you to always look for him as I do. I wronged him, but have regretted it for years. That is all, except to tell you that my will leaves you as my heir in case he doesn't turn up. If he does, everything goes to him, excepting an annuity and a junior partnership in the mills, which goes to you. Naturally you will eventually get the rest."

"Oh. thank you, grandfather, but I'm sure, sir, I'd much rather have you than the money or the mills!"

"I know that, my boy," replied Mr. Alliston, rising and placing his hand affectionately on the boy's shoulder; "but one never knows what may happen, although I feel young and hope to live a long time yet." And he started pacing the room again.

"Have you a picture of my father?" asked Jack.

"No, in my anger I destroyed every photograph I had."

"Supposing, sir, he didn't come for a long time, after—after you—" And he hesitated on the words.

"You mean after my death," finished Mr. Alliston. "Well, of course, he will have changed with the years, but you couldn't mistake him. He is big and fair, with blue eyes, and, besides, he has one distinctive mark. When he was a little fellow he was playing with one of my guns, and it went off accidentally, blowing off the little finger of his left hand.

"Well, we'll talk no more about it just now. You had better get ready to leave, and I will go along to the railway-station with you. While you get your things, I will ring for Harris, and send word for the motor to be brought round, and also for James to take your luggage."

"Thanks, sir; I won't be long," replied Jack, and turned to go as his grandfather moved to the hall.

The impassive Harris who appeared to answer Mr. Alston's summons, wore a very different expression on his face than he had a few moments previously when he had listened behind the curtains.

A little later, Jack and Mr. Alliston were motoring into the village, and, catching the up-train, Jack returned to Crowestoft School.

THE SECOND CHAPTER.   Mr. William Saunders, alias Jim Ford, alias Jim Carson, Plans a Coup—He Takes a Journey.

MR. WILLIAM SAUNDERS was evidently in a good humour if the chuckles which he emitted at intervals were any indication of his state of mind.

He was reading a letter, and the contents were undoubtedly of a pleasing nature.

He was sitting in a dilapidated armchair in a room furnished in a most frugal manner. The one begrimed window which it contained looked out on a squalid courtyard from which came a medley of noises. They were caused by a number of dirty children amusing themselves by the entertaining occupation of tormenting a mangy yellow cur.

Their game was interrupted at frequent intervals by a general free fight, and the profane interference of a couple of slatternly women when the fight waxed too hot.

Mr. Saunders seemed oblivious to the pandemonium, for he leaned back in his chair, and his audible remarks bore no reference to the racket below.

"I guess it's about time to make a move," he said, "a few more weeks to let this thing lose its new look"—and he held up a bandaged left hand and glanced at it—"and then I'll start things going. If I hadn't gone broke on that rubber deal, I could have made a different plan. Harris and James are getting impatient, too, so I think I had better run down to Alliston and see what this good news is which Harris says he's got."

He was a big man, and as he rose to his feet and paced the room he walked with the swing of a mountaineer. He was not unpleasing in appearance, but the keen observer saw that his eyes were set a bit too close together. Where he came from no one knew. He had no friends, and his landlady was practically the only person he spoke to. Certainly, no one would realise that the man pacing the room was the same man who, as James Ford, had swept meteor-like across the financial sky of the City a few years previously. James Ford had come from America, and had speculated heavily on the Exchange, making and losing large fortunes. He had eventually developed into one of the biggest operators on the "Street," and when rubber was booming had sunk his entire fortune. The market went against him, and he dropped

18

everything. He had disappeared as suddenly as he had come, and no one knew where he had gone. Reappearing quietly as William Saunders, he had nursed his remaining funds carefully, and, enlisting the services of two clever rascals, he started to carry out a plan which he had formed many years previously.

He turned and entered the adjoining room, from which he presently reappeared with a coat and cap on. Putting the letter which he had been reading in his pocket, he went out, closing the door and locking it carefully after him.

He threaded his way through a filthy littered alley, and catching a 'bus to Waterloo, climbed to the top and lit a cigarette. He was not dressed shabbily, but his clothes struck the observer as those of a man who had come down in the world, and still retained some of his belongings. That impression was just what he desired to create. As he smoked his cigarette and glanced casually at the passing traffic, his fellow-passengers would doubtless have been horrified had they known the tenor of his thoughts, and he laughed to himself as that reflection crossed his mind.

On his arrival at Waterloo he booked a first-class return to Alliston, and secured a carriage to himself. When the train arrived at Alliston, a tall man, with black moustache and beard, stepped from the carriage into which a smooth-shaven man had entered at Waterloo. He took the road leading away from the village, and swung along at a smart pace in the direction of Alliston Hall. As he approached the house he turned from the road, and, climbing the wall which separated the grounds from it, he made his way, as though familiar with the surroundings, in a circuitous manner through the trees, and came out near the stables. Dusk had already fallen, and he stepped confidently to the stable entrance. He gave a low whistle as he entered, and a door opposite opened. He moved over to it, and addressed the man who confronted him.

"Well, James, how goes it?" he asked coolly, closing the door and seating himself on a box.

The man who had opened the door had been standing silently, waiting for him to speak. He was a surly-looking fellow, and his voice, when he answered, showed him to be in a bad temper.

"'Ow goes it? A nice question to arsk. You 'ires me to go in on a job, an' then leave me down 'ere lookin' arter a lot o' blessed 'orses!"

"Steady, James, steady; you'll be losing that charming temper of yours. Now, keep cool, and tell me what is the trouble."

"Trouble? The trouble is he want's ter know when you intend ter make a move. I'm sick of it, I am!"

"You go and tell Harris I am here, and to slip out for a few moments," cut in Saunders icily, "and then I'll talk to you."

The man sullenly went to do as he was bid, muttering angrily as he went.

He returned a few moments later, and they sat in silence, until the door was pushed open and Harris entered.

"Well, Harris, I got your letter and came right down," remarked Saunders as he entered.

"Yes, I've got good news. It gives us all the facts we needed, but makes a complication—to my mind."

"Complication! How do you mean?"

And the "faithful" Harris proceeded to repeat the conversation he had overheard the day previously.

"His telling the boy makes it all the better," remarked Saunders, when the tale was finished.

"I don't think so." replied Harris. "Identification marks, when not genuine, are always dangerous."

"Nonsense! I saw his often enough to know just what it looked like, and I had mine taken off in exactly the same manner. It helps things a lot. The boy will look for that the first thing when the long-lost father turns up, and it will create confidence immediately, especially as I know now, from what you overheard, just how it was done." And he chuckled.

"I wrote out the whole conversation, so you could read it over," said Harris, passing him an envelope.

"Wot I want ter know, is 'ow long this 'ere foolin's goin' ter keep on before we starts?" growled James, who up to now had remained silent.

"Just as long as I decide it will," answered Saunders. "Your part is to obey orders, and not interfere with my business."

"Yer can't treat me like that," sullenly answered James. "We be all in on this, an' it ain't no tea-party game, either."

"If you try any threats, you will discover pretty quick how I can treat you!" snapped Saunders.

"How long before you think you will make a move?" asked Harris, interrupting the wrangle; while James subsided, muttering.

"About two months, perhaps less. I want the recent appearance of this operation to disappear, and I am applying some stuff to help it along. It may be only a month. At any rate, you fellows keep ready for the word, and I will let you know. Don't mess up your parts, and keep cool, no matter what happens. I won't risk coming down here until I come for business, so don't forget. If anything turns up in the meantime, Harris, write me to the same address. I'll have to make a move soon," he added, rising to leave, "as funds are getting jolly low."

And the conference of these unpleasant scoundrels broke up.

Saunders returned by the path he had come, and, catching the evening train to London, stepped out at Waterloo, the smooth-shaven man he had been when he had started.

THE THIRD CHAPTER.   The Murder of Charles Alliston—
The Plan to Outwit the Police—Saunders Escapes to America.

SOME six weeks later a man descended from the night train at Alliston. Leaving the village, he struck off toward the Hall, and climbed the wall as he had on his previous visit. Circuiting through the trees, he arrived at the stables, and a soft whistle gained him admittance.

"Is it you, James?" whispered the new-comer in the darkness.

"Yes," came an answering whisper.

"Did Harris get my letter?"

"Yes; everything is ready," came the voice in reply.

"Tip him off, then, that I am here, and tell him to smuggle me in past the maids when he can."

"All right." And a shuffling sound indicated the movement of the invisible person.

Saunders—for it was he—felt around until his hand felt a box, and, seating himself, he sat motionless until he heard returning footsteps.

"Harris says you'll 'ave to wait 'ere until the maids go ter bed," whispered James as he entered.

"All right. Don't talk; it's dangerous." And again silence reigned.

More than an hour passed before the watchers heard footsteps and a whispered curse as their owner stumbled in the dark.

"Is that you, Harris?" whispered Saunders, as a dark figure appeared in the doorway.

"Yes," came the answer. "Come along."

"All right. Be sure and have everything ready, so I can get the motor out quickly," Saunders added, turning to James. "And don't forget to obliterate any footprints I may have made behind the stable."

"I'll attend to it all right," growled the surly James. And Saunders departed silently in Harris's wake.

Lifting the latch of the side-door noiselessly, they stole silently through a long passage and emerged into the main hall.

"He's in the library now, having a peg," whispered Harris. "Come into the drawing-room and do your changing."

"All right; go ahead." And Saunders followed as Harris opened a door on the opposite side of the Hall, and closed it silently after them.

"Where are the shoes?" whispered Saunders.

"I put them under a sofa. Wait here until I get them." And Harris crept on his hands and knees across the room, returning presently with a parcel.

"Are you going to put them on now?" he asked as he returned.

"No; you keep them here ready. On second thoughts, you'd better come out in the hall. The old bird might put up a fight, and if you hear me whistle you will know I need help. Come at once if you do, for we can't waste any time, and there mustn't be any signs of a struggle in the room.

"Very well, I'll be on hand."

"Now, let me get everything clear," whispered Saunders. "You say when I open the door there are heavy curtains inside."

"Yes; and I oiled the hinges to-day."

"Good! Then on the left as I enter the room is a fireplace?"

"Yes."

"And you say he is sitting before it, reading."

"Yes."

"Is he on the left or the right of it?"

"On the left. He is in one of the big chairs, and as you enter, his back will be towards you, and the high back of the chair will also hide you."

"All right; then I'll get along. Don't hesitate to come at once if you hear me whistle."

A barely perceptible noise, and the following disappearance of the streak of light which shone from under the library door told the listening Harris that Saunders had accomplished his purpose."

He entered the room nervously, and peered through the gloom.

"Hurry up!" came Saunders's voice, in a whisper, and Harris, glancing fiercely over his shoulder, moved across and handed Saunders the shoes he had brought.

Silence reigned as the murderer took off his own and put the others on, and a moment later, pushing up the window, he slid out and disappeared across the lawn. He kept on until he came to a gravel path, where he turned and walked back to the library, following the same course.

"That will puzzle some of their smart men," he chuckled, as he climbed through the window and sat down to remove the shoes he had just utilised. Be sure and clean those well in the morning, and put them back where you got them," he added, passing them to Harris.

"And for Heaven's sake see there is no mud around the floor!"

"I'll clean up thoroughly after you go," said Harris, passing him the shoes he had just removed from the dead man's feet.

Saunders put on the fresh pair, and, tying his own— which had been lying on the floor all this time around his waist by the laces, he again rose and slipped out of the window.

"Pass out the body!" he whispered back to Harris, and Harris carefully lifted it from the chair, dragged it over to the window, and heaved it on to Saunders's waiting shoulders.

"Don't forget what I said," he cautioned Harris, as he was leaving. "and don't make a move of any kind until you hear from me. Remember, it is a big stake, and it pays to go slow and not make any mistakes. Keep your eye on James, and don't let him do anything foolish. I'm sorry we let him in on it, but we've got to put up with him now. Goodnight!"

"Goodnight! I'll be careful," replied Harris, leaving the window open, and starting to clean up the room.

Saunders was carrying a heavy load, and, big man though he was, he staggered under the weight. He went in the direction he had taken on the previous trip, and, reaching the edge of the gravelled walk, deposited his burden on the grass beside it. He sat down and removed the shoes he was wearing. He put them on the dead man and carefully laced them up. Untying his own from around his waist, he put them on. He then lifted himself to his feet, taking care that his own shoes rested on the gravel.

He followed the gravelled path around until he came to the garage.

"Are you here, James?" he whispered.

"Yes," came the answer.

"Is everything ready?"

"Yes. Did things go all right?"

"Splendid; not a hitch. Have you fixed the door so it looks smashed?"

"Yes; I broke the lock and split the wood around it as well."

"Good! You'd better duck now, and I'll be going. Don't lose your head, James, and be patient; the reward will well repay you."

"Oh, I'll be patient! Only I do likes action, an' I do 'ates 'orses."

"It won't be for long. Now go! I want to get away."

And James disappeared in the dark.

Saunders started the engine, and, jumping in, drove away in the night. The murmur of the almost noiseless engine sounded like fifty engines in his tense condition.

Mr. Saunders was a very clever criminal, probably one of the cleverest who had ever "honoured" England, but he made four mistakes that night.

THE FOURTH CHAPTER.   Breakfast at Lord Raymonde's — They Hear the News—Sexton Blake Investigates.

"THERE have been hundreds of criminals who were never caught or were never even suspected. I claim that a really clever, educated man who keeps ahead of the times can commit a crime and make his retreat without leaving a trace,"

The speaker was Sir Walter Hall, and he was addressing a group of men who were enjoying an early breakfast before leaving for the shoot, Lord Raymonde being the host.

There were half a dozen of them—Lord Raymonde, the host; Dr. Thornton, the famous nerve specialist; Colonel Tucker, the well-known explorer; his son, who was in the Guards; Sir Walter Hall, sportsman and J.P.; and Sexton Blake, the famous detective.

The conversation had turned on crime and the criminal, started by young Tucker, probably in order to hear Sexton Blake's opinion.

"What is your opinion, Blake?" asked the host, laughing. "Do you agree with Sir Walter, or will your ideas put him to rout?"

Blake smiled, and said:

"I don't know that I ought to join in this discussion; but although it is true that many crimes go unpunished and their perpetrators unsuspected, I hold that no criminal is clever enough to commit a crime from its inception to its completion without a single mistake, and that a specialist in crime, given a fair opportunity, can discover that mistake and eventually find the criminal."

"Of course I know, Mr. Blake, you have never lost a case," replied Sir Walter. "But look at the hundreds of cases that go undiscovered by the best men at Scotland Yard."

"I know, Sir Walter," answered Blake, smiling modestly at the first part of Sir Walter's remark; "but you will find, as scientific methods are adopted more and more, that the percentage of captured criminals will increase. The science of crime is the most embracing science in the world. It includes a thorough knowledge of every other science, language; and country known, and the man who follows that profession to-day must keep abreast of the times, for, unfortunately, the criminal of to-day is an educated, clever man and his methods are almost in advance of science. The specialist must therefore be even in advance of the criminal, and follow the psychology of his mind." And Blake leaned back and sipped his coffee.

"I agree with Mr. Blake," joined in young Tucker. "By Jove, I'd like to see you work on a case!" he added enthusiastically.

"I'd be glad to have you any time." laughed Blake.

"You may be right in your contention," continued Sir Walter stubbornly, "but I can't believe there is no crime that can't be unravelled. I'd like to wager on it," he added.

"I'm afraid you'd lose your money if you wagered it with Mr. Blake," joined in Dr. Thornton and Colonel Tucker almost simultaneously.

A general laugh went round the table at their remark, for both of them were rare speakers, and had been apparently engrossed with their own thoughts.

At that part of the conversation the door opened, and the butler entered. Requesting a word with his master, he bent down and whispered in the latter's ear, while Lord Raymonde's brows went up with astonishment. Nodding and dismissing the man, he turned to his guests.

"By Jove, you fellows, what do you think of this on top of our conversation? Jackson tells me that a neighbour of mine, Charles Alliston, the wealthy mill-owner, was murdered in his grounds last night."

A chorus of ejaculations greeted the remark.

"Do you know any details?" they asked.

"No; just the bare statement. I suppose you will look into it, Blake?" he added, addressing the detective.

"I wouldn't mind. But, of course, I suppose the inspector from the Yard will prefer me to wait until he gets there. However, it might be worth while going over, and I think, if you will excuse me from shooting this morning, I will do so. It might prove a mystery which can't be unravelled," he laughed, turning to Sir Walter.

"By George, I'd like to go with you! May I, Mr. Blake?" asked young Tucker,

"With pleasure. I'll get the car, and we'll go over right away. By the way, Lord Raymonde, how far is it?"

"About eight miles. I'll send one of the grooms to show you the way."

"Thanks! That will be splendid," answered Blake.

There was a general rising from the table, all discussing the news they had heard, excepting the great detective, who knit his brows in deep thought.

Blake and his companion were soon on their way, and as the detective had never been over the road before he took a mental photograph of the topography of the passing country-side the while he carried on a desultory conversation with Tucker. As they arrived at the gate's of Alliston Hall he brought the car to a stop. Leaving it in charge of the groom, he and Tucker proceeded on foot to the house.

The door was opened by the butler, who seemed much affected by his master's death.

As he ushered them into the hall, he said, addressing Blake, who had passed him his card:

"I don't know that I ought to admit you to the library, sir, until Inspector Thomas arrives. He might not like it." And the admirable Harris radiated sorrowful regret.

"It makes no difference," answered Blake. "By the way, what is your name?'' he added.

"Harris, sir."

"I see. Well, Harris, I don't suppose you will object if I look around outside?"

"Oh, no, sir! I will show you round myself."

"I won't take you away from your duties, Harris. My companion, Mr. Tucker, will accompany me."

"Very good, sir," the man replied, as Blake moved toward the door.

"Oblige me by strolling around in front, please, Tucker. I won't be long, and will explain my reason later. If Harris appears, engage him in conversation, and hold him some way until I return," murmured Blake hurriedly, as he strolled casually around the corner of the house.

"Right!" replied Tucker, catching his meaning, and pleased at his inclusion at the detective's actions. "I'll hold him!"

Blake strolled slowly on until he saw the open window. Walking quickly along the side of the house, he looked in, and, seeing the body stretched on a couch, knew it was the room Harris had refused to allow them to enter. Looking at the ground, he perceived the footprints leading from the window, and followed them until he came to the gravelled walk. Three times the detective paused, and took his mould from his pocket, and on reaching the walk he used it a fourth time.

"Inspector Thomas would be wild if he knew," murmured Blake, as he followed the gravelled walk around to the front.

Tucker was engaged in an animated conversation with Harris, and winked at Blake as he came up.

"Harris was looking for you, Mr. Blake, but I told him you had just strolled around the grounds. He wanted to go and assist you, but I told him you could find your way."

"Oh, yes!" answered Blake. "It was very good of you, Harris,"—turning to the man—"but I saw all I desired. Has Mr. Alliston any children or relatives?" he continued.

"One grandson, sir—Master Jack. I wired for him, and he will arrive at ten-thirty. Inspector Thomas also comes by that train, I think."

"Ah, very well. Harris! Mr. Tucker and I will sit here, and wait until Master Jack arrives." He seated himself on a garden bench in front, and Tucker joined him.

"Did you find anything of interest?" inquired the latter.

"I can't tell you. I want to hear the whole story, and I didn't care to ask the details until the inspector arrives. We'll wait until then."

"Right! I'm immensely interested!" replied Tucker, as he lit a cigarette.

Meanwhile, Harris had re-entered the house, and it is to be regretted Blake couldn't hear his remarks.

"I don't care for all Scotland Yard, but that man means trouble. He finds facts from nothing—curse him! I'll stop him, if I have to kill him!"

And he shook his fist in the direction of the unconscious detective.

THE FIFTH CHAPTER.   Arrival of Inspector Thomas and Jack— Inspector Forms a Theory—So Does Blake—Blake Takes Case for Jack.

BLAKE and Tucker smoked on the terrace for half an hour, until they perceived a trap coming up the drive.

"Here comes Inspector Thomas now!" remarked Blake, rising. "Let us go and meet him."

They strolled over to the trap as it stopped, and Inspector Thomas, accompanied by a tall boy, descended.

"I didn't expect to see you here, Blake," remarked the inspector, in a surprised tone, as he alighted.

"It is purely an accident," replied Blake. "I am staying for a few days, shooting with Lord Raymonde, whose place is near, and, hearing of the matter, I ran over."

"What do you make of it?" asked the inspector sharply.

"Oh, I have awaited your arrival! I didn't care to do anything until you came. In fact, I haven't even heard the story from the butler yet."

"Ah," remarked the inspector, and his manner thawed a little, "I'm glad you waited! By the way, this is Master Jack Alliston, who is a grandson of Mr. Alliston." And the boy, whose face indicated great grief, shook hands with Blake. "We came down on the same train," added the inspector.

Blake introduced Tucker, and the party moved into the house, where Harris received them.

"You'd better not come along," said the inspector, addressing Jack. "I'd wait, if I were you, until after the examination."

"Oh, no; I must come!" replied the boy appealingly. "Grandfather and I—"

But he choked on the words, and turned away.

"Come along!" broke in Blake. "It won't be any worse than sitting alone in your room."

"Now, Harris," said Inspector Thomas pompously, "tell me all you know about this unfortunate affair before we go into the library!"

"Well, sir," replied Harris. "I went to call the master this morning, and found his bed hadn't been slept in. I was a bit worried at the discovery, and came down at once to the library. When I opened the door I noticed the window was up, and the room empty, just as I was going over to the window I saw James, the coachman, sir, coming across the lawn in a hurry. He was very agitated, and I asked him what was the matter. He said he had found the master's body under the trees, and that there had been murder. I left the room, and went around to where the body lay. It was as he said, sir, for there was a large wound in the shoulder. We lifted it up, and carried it into the library. James said, sir, that the garage had been broken into, and the motor taken. I then telegraphed for you, sir."

"It seems hardly probable that the garage could be broken open, and the motor taken, without anyone hearing the noise," interrupted the inspector. "But, however, we will go into the library, and have a look round. In the meantime, send for James!"

"Very well, sir!"

And Harris went to call the coachman, while the party moved into the library.

Jack gave a cry as he saw the body, and fell on his knees beside it, but Blake put his hand on the boy's shoulder, and said:

"Steady, my boy; keep up your courage. I know it is hard, but you will need all your strength during the next few days."

The boy's eyes hardened as he dragged himself to his feet.

"I'll find his murderer, if it takes me all my life; and when I do—"

And he seemed to grow older as he stood erect, and clenched his hands.

They went over to the body, and the inspector examined it first before permitting Blake to do so.

Inspector Thomas was a pompous man, and did not entertain very warm feelings for Blake, since the latter had beaten him on several cases. His manner showed he would have preferred the detective's absence, but Blake ignored it. His all-seeing eyes, however, darted around the room, taking in everything.

Harris returned with James, and they stood inside the door, awaiting the inspector's wishes.

"Has anything been disturbed?" he asked.

"No, sir." replied Harris. "James and I carried the body in, and I wouldn't allow anyone near the room."

"What time did you last see the deceased last night?"

"He rang about ten, sir, and I brought him a whisky-and-soda. He told me I could go then, and, after locking up, I retired."

"Where was he sitting?"

"In that chair on the left of the fireplace, sir."

"The window was closed of course, when you brought him his drink?"

"Oh, yes; sir!"

"There must be some footprints outside with this muddy weather?" remarked the inspector, moving to the window.

"Yes, there are, sir, and I kept everybody away from them." answered Harris.

And Sexton Blake glanced sharply at the man as he heard him.

"Ah, that was wise! What do you make of this, Mr. Blake?" asked the inspector, after examining the footprints.

"I haven't formed any theory yet," answered Blake.

"Looks pretty clear to me." said the inspector. "We'll just follow them out to where the body was found. Here's a line of footprints approaching the window," he continued, as they walked along "and the same prints going back again. Here is a single line leaving the window, and not returning. Mr. Alliston was found at the end of this line, and, as I expected."—measuring the prints and comparing them with the shoes on the dead man's feet— "they were made by the deceased. Very clear, I think. Someone approached the window, rapped, and the deceased opened it. The caller evidently said something which induced Mr. Alliston to accompany him, and the man murdered him under the trees. Let us go to the garage, and have a look there," he continued.

And the others followed him.

As they returned, and arrived the second time at the spot where the body had been picked up, the inspector made a closer examination of the ground. He saw a mark which interested him, and approached to examine it, but Harris accidentally trod on it with his heel, and in the soft mud it was obliterated.

Harris was again favoured with a scrutinising look from Blake, but in the profusion of his apologies to the inspector he did not perceive it.

Sexton Blake already had a mould of that mark which had interested the inspector in his pocket.

After the inspector had jotted down some notes, the party returned to the library.

"I'll send a constable up here, and I want you to leave everything untouched," the inspector said, addressing Harris. "I'll send another man along, and you can take the trap and go with him in search of the motor," he added to James. "I don't think it will be far away—probably only a blind. It looks like a clear case," he continued, turning to Blake. "Doubtless one of the men who worked in the mills, who had a grievance. I'll investigate that point," he added, as he turned and strutted to the door.

"I think we had better get along, too," said Blake, turning to Tucker. "Good-bye!" he continued, holding out his hand to Jack. "Keep up your courage!"

"Can I speak to you privately, Mr. Blake, before you go?" interrupted the boy.

"Yes; certainly! Come out to the car, and we can talk undisturbed."

Excusing himself to Tucker, he led the way outside, followed by Harris' angry eyes.

"Now, what is it?" he asked, as they leaned over the car.

"Won't you take this case, and help me find grandfather's murderer, Mr. Blake?" said the boy. "The police are so slow, and I know you will find him if you take it on."

"I am pretty busy at present." replied Blake, "and, although the case presents some very interesting features, I am afraid—"

"Oh, don't say you can't!" broke in the boy. "Please take it on!"

And he grasped Blake's arm in his earnestness.

"All right, my boy, I will. I'll go back to town to-day and start on it. Are you returning to school?"

"Yes; I will go back and finish the term. There are only a few more weeks, and I know grandfather would wish it."

"What school is it?"

"Crowestoft."

"Ah, yes; I know it, very well. I will communicate with you there. By the way, have you no other relatives?" asked Blake.

"Well, I hardly know whether my father is alive or not. Grandfather only told me about him the day I returned to school for this term."

And he proceeded to tell Blake what Mr. Alliston had told him.

"Have you a photograph of him?" asked Blake.

"No. sir. Grandfather destroyed them all when he was angry."

"How will you recognise him if he turns up? Will the family

lawyers know him?"

"No; they wouldn't. Mr. Burton would have, but since he died grandfather has had his business done by a London firm, and that is since my father went away. But grandfather described him to me. He is big and fair, and, besides, he has one distinguishing mark—the little finger on the left hand is missing. Grandfather said he lost it by the accidental explosion of a gun."

"Ah!" said Blake. "I see! Well, have patience, my boy, and keep up your courage."

"I will, sir, and thank you so much for helping me."

"Oh, that's all right!" smiled Blake, and beckoned to Tucker, who stood waiting.

"Well, it seems a pretty clear case, as the inspector says." remarked the latter, as they drove away.

"It would seem so on the face of it," smiled Blake, but the great detective's remarks to himself as he entered his room to pack his bags were very different.

"Which goes to prove my statement," he muttered, "that no criminal, no matter how clever, can execute a crime from its inception to its completion without a single mistake; and the unknown man in this case has made four."

THE SIXTH CHAPTER.   Blake Follows Up a Clue Baffled— Light on the Matter—Tinker and Pedro take up the Trail.

"I'M deucedly sorry you are breaking your trip short, Blake, but I suppose if you must, you must. However, we will be here for some time yet, so if you get a chance, run down again," And as he spoke, Lord Raymonde held out his hand.

"Thanks!" said Blake, taking it. "I've enjoyed myself, but matters have arisen which make it imperative that I should run up to London; but you may see me again sooner than you think," he laughed, climbing into the big car, and taking the wheel. "So I only say au revoir."

"That's right, come whenever you can. We'll be delighted," answered his host, as Blake started away after waving his hand to the rest of the assembled guests who stood on the steps.

They would have been surprised if they had seen the big car turning in entirely the opposite direction from London as it gained the road, and go spinning at a smart pace towards Alliston Hall. It kept steadily on, passing it at high speed, and the detective did not slacken his pace until he had covered a score of miles. It was early in the afternoon, and he desired to test a theory before driving on to London.

He pulled up at each village through which he passed, and made an inquiry, but did not gain the information he wanted until he had covered a good eighty miles. As he descended a steep hill with a stone bridge at the bottom, he saw a number of farmers congregated together, examining some object in the bed of the stream. Looking down, he saw a wrecked motor-car, and brought his own to a standstill.

"Looks like a bad smash," he remarked to the crowd who stood looking on.

"That it is, sir," said one. "Jones here, saw it as he was driving over the bridge. It was half in the water, and half out, and almost hidden by the tree."

"Have you found the driver?" asked Blake.

"No, sir; not a sign."

"You won't, either," said Blake drily; and they looked at him in astonishment. "You'd better turn it over to the police."

"We've sent for the constable already." replied the man.

"That's right; he will doubtless soon find the owner. How far is the railway-station from here?" added the detective.

"About a mile further on," replied the man.

"Thanks!" And Blake drove on.

The detective drew a blank. He spent several hours interviewing every stationmaster within the greatest possible radius which his theory embraced, but the answers had all been the same.

"No, they hadn't sold a ticket that morning to a man, nor, in fact, to anyone. Three had been sold by one man in the afternoon, but they were returns, and were to local residents whom he knew well. No, no goods train had stopped—one had run through, but it was a non-stop train. What time? About eleven the previous night."

And Blake knew his man couldn't have caught it so early. It would be one o'clock, at least, before he would be able to get that far from Alliston.

The great detective was plainly puzzled as he turned the car and headed for London, and sat absorbed in thought as he drove the big machine on its two-hour run.

"Why, of course," he muttered, as he turned into Baker Street, "why didn't I think of that? Let me see, Liverpool is the nearest. I will send Tinker to look that up,"

.   .   .   .   .

"Did you have a good time, guv'nor?" asked Tinker, stretching his arms and yawning as the noise of Blake's entrance awoke him from the enjoyment of a sleep in a big chair before the fire.

"Fine! Anything new?"

"No, not a thing, guv'nor. I say, you are, muddy!"

"Yes, I was driving fast," laughed Blake. "Stir yourself, my boy, I've got work for you to do."

"Good! I just wanted something."

"Well, you'll get it this time, if I'm not mistaken."

"Is it a new case, guv'nor?"

"Yes." And Blake explained the facts to him. "I want you to go to Farnham and start from there," said the detective, as he finished his explanation. "It didn't occur to me this afternoon while I was there, but I feel sure the fugitive would have another car waiting for him. Pick up the trail, and follow it. I think you will find it will lead to a seaport, probably Liverpool; but make sure. Find out all you can, and wire me. I'll look up some other matters here, and you should be back by to-morrow night. Don't waste a moment, as time is valuable."

"Right, guv'nor!" replied Tinker, jumping to his feet. "Will I take Pedro?" he asked, as the great beast entered and greeted Blake.

"Yes, if you wish. He might be useful in picking up the trail. You can get a train in an hour, so you'll have to hurry."

"Right!" And Tinker hastened away to pack a bag.

•   •   •   •   •

Tinker found the wrecked car the next morning, as Blake had said, and, hiring another from the local garage, he started to pick up the trail. On reaching Blakely, he stopped at the inn and made inquiries. He discovered that the boots boy had heard a motor going through the previous morning as he got up.

"What time was it?"

"About four o'clock."

And Tinker hastened on.

Following the trail on the information gained, Tinker found it headed steadily in the direction of Liverpool. As he arrived there, he paid the driver, and betook himself first to the docks, he discovered that the Caronia had sailed at ten the previous morning for New York, and, going to her dock, he finally located a man still on duty who was there when she sailed.

"Were you near the gangway when the Caronia left?" asked Tinker, slipping the man a half-sovereign.

"Yes, that I was, young sir."

"Were there any late arrivals? Did you see any passengers coming up just before she left?"

"Come to think on it now, I did," replied the man, spitting. "A motor drove up, and a big man got out. He didn't do no more than catch it, either," he added. "Was he a friend of yourn?"

"Yes; I wanted very much to see him before he left," replied Tinker truthfully; "but I see I have missed him."

And, thanking the man, he hastened away to a telegraph-office, the faithful Pedro trotting beside him.

Tinker sent a long telegram to Blake. He gave his address at an hotel, and proceeded there to have lunch and await an answer. He had just finished, and was amusing himself by watching the people around him, when the waiter handed him the expected message. Tearing it open, he read:

"Return at once."

THE SEVENTH CHAPTER.   Tinker Leaves for New York— The Passenger from the Caronia—Tinker on the Trail.

"I WANT you to get ready at once to leave for New York," said Blake, as Tinker finished his report.

"Oh, that will be splendid!" said the boy eagerly, "Does Pedro go, too?"

"I'm afraid not," smiled Blake. "I looked up the sailings to-day while you were gone," he continued, "and find the Caronia is a seven-day boat. The Mauretania leaves in the morning, and docks about four hours before the Caronia, so you will be there in time to watch the passengers go ashore. I will give you a letter to Detective Carter, of New York, and he will arrange for you to get a position at the gangway as they descend. I have procured a large plan of the city, and am also giving you a letter to the manager of the Hotel Belmont. It is a magnificent hotel, but as I want you to adopt the role of a young gentleman of leisure travelling for amusement, it will be necessary for you to stay at a place of that description. When you take your place at the gangway as the passengers descend, stand so you will be on their left, and look at the left hands of everyone as they come down. If you see one with the little finger of his left hand missing, follow him, and see where he goes, keeping me advised by cable, and don't lose sight of him. Detective Carter will let you have a couple of men to assist you."

"I will see him if he gets off, and if I do, I won't lose sight of him," replied Tinker.

"Well, keep your eyes open, and don't get into trouble. New York is a bad place in parts, and you may find your man will patronise these parts. Keep your revolver handy, and use it if you are attacked. Detective Carter will give you an authority which will be of assistance to you. Now get some sleep, and be fresh for the trip."

.   .   .   .   .

Tinker had often been in New York, but the promise of a race against time with the Caronia filled him with a pleasurable excitement. Blake had given him his final instructions, and had taken his departure, and Tinker, proud of the responsibility, vowed to be worthy of the trust as the great steamer left the dock.

He enjoyed every minute of the trip, and his frank, sunny ways made him a general favourite on board. As they sailed up the harbour,

38

past the towering Statue of Liberty which stands at the front gate of the New World, Tinker indulged his interest in everything he saw, for they had passed the Caronia in the night, and he knew he would reach her dock before she landed her passengers.

He hastened ashore, getting through the Customs as quickly as possible, and, taking a taxi, proceeded at once to Mulberry Street.

Detective Carter was the most famous detective in America, and Tinker was anxious to see the man who was only second to Sexton Blake. He found Carter in his office, and presented his letter. The detective read it, and looked at Tinker with a searching gaze.

He was a smooth-shaven man, with keen grey eyes, and Tinker thought to himself that he didn't look unlike Sexton Blake.

"You're pretty young to be doing such responsible work, aren't you?" he asked, smiling.

"I don't know, sir. Mr. Blake has entrusted me with some important things before now, and they were handled to his satisfaction." replied Tinker modestly.

"I don't doubt it, my boy," answered Carter, holding out his hand. "Just let me know what I can do for you. I will be glad to oblige you for Sexton Blake's sake, even though he has beaten me before now. I reckon he is a great detective, and you are indeed fortunate to get your training under him."

"He is, sir!" replied Tinker, his eyes shining with enthusiasm. "He has been awfully good to me. Could you let me have two men?" he continued. "I want to catch the Caronia before she docks, and may need them to shadow a man."

"Certainly; with pleasure. I'll send two of my plainclothes men with you." And, ringing the bell, he gave instructions to the patrolman who entered to send in the men he wanted.

He introduced Tinker to the men, Hill and O'Hara, as they entered, and said:

"You will go with this gentleman, and consider yourselves under his instructions. He represents the famous Sexton Blake, and I want you to show him we can do things here as well as they can do them in London." And he smiled at Tinker, while the men looked at the lad with added respect.

Tinker felt a glow of pride as he saw the power of his benefactor's name even in a foreign land.

"Thank you, Mr. Carter," he said, holding out his hand. "I will get along now to the Belmont and leave my bags. You had better come with me," he said, turning to the men, "and we can go right down to the Caronias dock from there."

The men saluted Carter and followed Tinker out to the taxi.

As they swung into Broadway, Tinker confessed to himself that he liked what he had so far seen of their methods. Tinker felt he was on his metal, for he knew they would watch every detail of his English methods.

Crossing Madison Square, where the commanding Tower throws its long shadow, and passing Martin's and the famous Flat Iron Building, they continued up Broadway—that unique world-known thoroughfare—until they reached Times Square. They swung into Forty-Second Street, past the magnificent Knickerbocker Hotel, and continued down, until the impressive Hotel Belmont reared its massive bulk to their right pulling up. Tinker saw opposite on one corner the busy Manhattan Hotel. Grand Central Station stretched away from the other, while on the fourth stood the old Grand Union, that Mecca of the new arrival.

He ungrudgingly admitted that the great city was attractive, and he looked forward to some interesting excursions, if his mission would permit.

A porter opened the door of the taxi, and, leaving the two plain-clothes men in the machine, he followed his luggage into the hotel. As he crossed the marble foyer he pulled Sexton Blake's letter from his pocket, and, asking for the manager, presented it. The manager shook hands warmly.

"Glad to know you, sir. Any friend of Sexton Blake's is always welcome here. Don't hesitate to ask for anything. I will be glad to oblige you in any way I can."

Tinker, as he thanked him for the offer, again glowed with pride in the thought that he was Blake's friend.

The manager instructed the clerk to give Tinker rooms looking out on Forty-Second Street; and again telling the lad to command him in any way he could, he hurried away.

Tinker signed his name in the register, and, getting the number of his room, sent up the boy with his luggage. He went out to the cab again, and telling the chauffeur to drive at once on the Caronia's dock, he settled back and thought over his plans, until they turned into Twenty-Third Street and headed for the dock.

They reached the Caronia's dock before she appeared in the river. He placed his men in convenient positions, and approaching one of the officials, by the use of Carter's name secured the privilege of standing at the gangway, which he wished. Leaning against the shed, which almost covered the wharf, he patiently waited until he saw the Caronia steam gracefully up the river and swing towards the dock. As she approached he closely scanned the passengers leaning over the rail, but got no hint of the identity of the man for whom he was looking.

When her cables were made secure and the gangway lifted up, he strolled carelessly over and took up his position. He knew he would create no suspicion in the mind of the man he wanted, as there were dozens of people crowding up to meet returning relatives and friends. Several people had descended, and, their left hands being exposed, he knew none of them was the one for whom he was looking. Glancing up, he saw a tall man, with black beard and moustache, descending, whose left hand was thrust carelessly in the pocket of his coat, while in his right he carried a bag.

Tinker's mind worked like lightning—he must get a glimpse of that hand. It wouldn't do to miss one, for if he did, it might be just the one he wanted. Lifting his hand to his head, he knocked his cap off, apparently by accident, and it fell on the gangway in front of the descending man. The man stopped and involuntarily removed his hand, stooping to pick it up as he did so. Tinker apologised and reached for it, but his heart gave a jump as he saw that the little finger of the man's hand was missing.

Signalling O'Hara to follow the quarry, he held his position for a few moments, and then joined Hill.

"Is that the man you are after?" asked Hill.

"I think so. Do you know him in New York?"

"No; I can't say I do. Of course, he's probably disguised; but I don't recognise him. Seems to know his way about," he added, as the man jumped into a taxi and instructed the driver where to go.

O'Hara secured another and followed, while Tinker and Hill followed him; and the little procession moved up Twenty-Third Street and turned up Broadway. Tinker and Hill kept the other two in sight, and saw them turn into Forty-Fourth Street. They saw their man descend and enter a small hotel, while another taxi ahead they rightly judged to be O'Hara's. Following it, they turned into Sixth Avenue, and it pulled up, awaiting their approach.

"You get out and watch the hotel," said Tinker to O'Hara as they stopped. "If he goes out, follow him. Hill can follow you, and bring me word where you go. I will relieve you at six and keep him in sight until midnight. In the meantime, send another man to follow me and take any message I wish to send to you, and you and Hill can relieve us again at midnight. Have the new man come to the Belmont, so I will know him, and be sure and come for me sharp at six," he added, turning to Hill.

O'Hara sprang out and strolled back to Forty-Fourth Street, while Hill followed him casually. Tinker returned to his hotel and cabled to Blake.

"GENTLEMAN to see you, sir!"

Tinker was lounging in the lobby of the Belmont before dining, and looked up as the porter spoke.

"Send him over here," he replied; and the man went away, to return with a large, good-natured looking man, who had, if not all, at least a portion of the map of Ireland on his face.

"Are you Mr. Sexton Blake's representative?" he asked in a broad Irish brogue as the man left; and Tinker nodded. "My name is Murphy," he continued, extending his hand, and his broad face broke into a smile, in which Tinker joined as he took the proffered hand. "The chief tells me I'm to report to you for instructions, sir; and, bedad, I'm glad to meet someone from the old land—for England is close to Ireland—and I'm right proud to work with a pardner of Sexton Blake's!" he finished, with an odd mixture of American words and Irish accent.

Tinker smiled.

"I want you to follow me to-night," he said. "I am relieving O'Hara at six, and want to keep a man in sight and if I need to send word of any kind to Detective Carter I will signal to you."

"Sure, I'll do that!" replied Murphy; and they arranged a code of signals.

Tinker made a hurried meal, and had just returned to the lobby when Hill entered.

"O'Hara is still in Forty-Fourth Street," he said. "The quarry hasn't come out since he got there."

"All right," replied Tinker; "we will go round." And, beckoning to Murphy, they passed out. The porter whistled up a taxi from the long rank which stood in front, and they were soon speeding up Broadway.

They stopped at the corner of Forty-Fourth Street, and Tinker strolled up towards the hotel which held his man. As he went along he saw O'Hara, who signalled that the man was still inside, and then hurried away in the other direction towards Sixth Avenue.

Tinker took up a sheltered position, and from where he stood could see everyone who entered and left the hotel, and also Murphy hovering further down the street.

"He seems to be lying low," he muttered to himself, after he had been keeping his solitary watch for over two hours. "I wonder if he's gone out a back way. It's hardly likely, for he can't be suspicious yet."

Almost as he spoke a tall man emerged from the hotel and hurried towards Sixth Avenue. Tinker recognised his quarry, and hastened after him, keeping him in sight. As he passed a large plate-glass window he could see the reflection of Murphy behind him, but it never occurred to him that his quarry might see him also, and, although not suspicious then of being followed, might recognise him if he saw him again later in the evening. Therein Tinker made a mistake which he regretted.

His man hurried across Sixth Avenue and walked down Forty-second Street. He then turned, and went up the steps leading to the Elevated Railway, and Tinker was close behind when the man bought a ticket. Pushing a coin under the window, Tinker followed him and gained the same car. He was just in time, for the doors closed almost at once, and looking through the window, he saw Murphy stamping with rage on the platform, and he knew the plain-clothes man had been too late to catch the train. No doubt he would follow on, but he would not know at which station they would get out. Tinker realised, with anxiety, that he must play a lone hand for at least the rest of that night. Settling himself in the corner of the carriage, he kept a surreptitious watch on his man, and as they stopped at Fourteenth Street he saw him rise. Tinker also rose, and followed him out.

"By golly!" he exclaimed. "I wish I knew this district better!" And he hurried anxiously along.

The chase continued over Fourteenth Street and down Avenue A, turning into the Bowery. Tinker knew that he was in a tough district, and his hand closed around his revolver as he walked. His man finally turned into a disreputable-looking saloon, and Tinker, taking up a position across the street, waited for his reappearance.

He could have enlisted the aid of a policeman by using Carter's name, but he didn't think it would do much good, as he had been told that the police in those districts were in league with the dens, and besides, as there was none in sight he couldn't leave his post to get one. Over an hour passed, and still his man remained in the saloon.

"I think I'll go in and see what has become of him. Perhaps I'll pick up some information, too," he said to himself; and crossing the street, pushed open the door. He descended half a dozen steps, and found himself in a brilliantly-lighted room. A bar ran along one side, and behind it, dispensing drinks, was one of the most villainous-looking men Tinker had ever seen. A number of small tables were scattered around, and the floor was covered with sawdust. A motley crowd filled the place, and it was hard to judge which had the most dissipated and evil-looking countenance. Several half-tipsy women in the company of tipsier men sat at the small tables, and here and there a maudlin song was bellowed forth.

Tinker made a rapid survey of the occupants of the room as he walked to the bar, but did not see his man.

He regretted entering the place, but realised he was now in for it, and that he must try and bluff it out. Leaning on the bar, he replied to the barkeeper's inquiry by ordering ginger-ale. A loud guffaw broke out close to his ear, and a coarse, drunken voice said:

"Listen to mother's boy! He wants ginger-ale! What's the matter, sonny? Did the milk run out?" And a general chorus of laughter greeted his sally.

Tinker made no reply, and reached for his drink, passing over the money as he did so.

The drunken bully, evidently not content with leaving him alone, sidled over to him and said:

"Better have a real drink, sonny!" And with the words reached for Tinker's glass and poured the contents on the floor.

Tinker realised he must be wary. He knew every man in the room would be against him, and, grinning good-naturedly, said:

"Why, certainly, I'll drink with you!" And as he spoke he edged towards the door.

He saw that if he could get a few feet nearer he could make a dash, and perhaps gain the street; but, glancing around, he noticed, with dismay, that for some unaccountable reason the number of people between himself and the door had increased considerably. Tinker did not know all the tricks of those Bowery dens.

He realised, though, that he was in for it, and gritting his teeth, resolved to keep his head, and shoot his way out if necessary. His hand closed on his revolver as he turned again to the bar, and as he did so he saw mischief in the leering eyes of the barkeeper.

"Give me a glass of ginger-ale," he said quietly.

"Certainly, sir!" said the bar-tender in a mockingly polite voice. He placed it on the bar a little distance up from where Tinker stood, and the lad, all unsuspecting of the particular trap laid for him, moved up to grasp it.

"Douse the glim!" shouted someone behind him; and as he heard the words Tinker pulled his revolver and swung round.

The lights went out as he did so, and he started to make for the door, when he felt the floor sink from under his feet, and he dropped, passing into unconsciousness as he struck the ground.

THE NINTH CHAPER.   Blake Anxious—Leaves for New York with Pedro—Where is Tinker?

BLAKE had received Tinker's cable and code saying he had spotted the man he was after and was shadowing him. He had cabled in reply, telling Tinker to keep him shadowed, and report progress until he heard further.

After he received Tinker's cable, he ran down to Alliston and had a look round, but nothing new had developed.

He had then gone to Crowestoft to see Jack, and questioned him in detail about his father and grandfather. He had also questioned him about the servants, and jotted down as a fact worth looking into the recent hiring of Harris and James.

Three days later, when he returned from Crowestoft, he firmly expected further word from Tinker. He was very worried when he found nothing, and still more so when a cable from Detective Carter informed him of Tinker's mysterious disappearance. He sat buried in thought, and at last roused himself.

"Poor boy!" he said. "I'm afraid I've sent him to his death!"

And Pedro seemed to realise there was something wrong, for he put his muzzle on Blake's knee and gazed sadly up into his eyes.

Blake sat pondering for some time, and finally rising, he rang for his landlady.

"Pack my steamer-trunk to-night! I'm going to book passage to New York, and will leave on Thursday or Friday. In the meantime, I shall be away over night, and will take a bag with me. Be sure and have everything ready when I return."

"Very good, sir! Will you be going on the evening train?"

"Yes; I will leave in an hour."

. . . . .

Crowestoft School is one of the old schools of England. Many famous men have had their characters moulded under its roof, and its venerable outlines were pleasantly dignified in the sunlight as Sexton Blake crossed the quad., and rang the bell of the doctor's residence.

Presenting his card to the trim maidservant who answered the door, he was ushered into a cosy drawing-room, to await the doctor's arrival.

"Ah, Mr. Blake!" he said, smiling genially as he entered. "You have returned soon!"

"Yes, doctor. I am leaving for New York on Thursday or Friday, and want to see young Alliston before I go, but desire to have a talk with you first."

"Certainly—certainly, Mr. Blake! What can I do for you?"

"I know young Alliston is still upset about the murder of his grandfather, and I also know that when the term is over he intends remaining at home instead of coming back. It will be very bad for him at his age to be there alone, brooding over the affair, and I want you to help me persuade him to promise, before I leave, that he will return."

"I entirely agree with you, Mr. Blake. I quite see your point. By the way, how are you making out in your investigations? It was a shocking affair!"

"It is a very complex case, doctor; but I hope to solve it before long. The investigation of crime is a good deal like making bread. You have to let it set for the yeast to rise. And that is exactly the condition this case is in. The yeast is rising, and I trust the baking will soon take place."

"I trust so," replied the doctor, smiling at the detective's simile. "I'll ring and send for Alliston now, and between us we will try and persuade him. I think you will have more weight with him than I will," added the doctor, as he resumed his seat after ringing. "He naturally listens to me; but he, as does every boy in the school, looks on you as the most wonderful genius alive." and his eyes twinkled.

"I also had a most wholesome respect for the doctor at my school," laughed Blake, as the door opened and Jack entered.

After a strenuous half-hour of persuasion, Jack passed his word to return, and Blake heaved a sigh of relief as he rose. He had his own reasons for desiring to keep Jack away from Alliston village. He foresaw danger for the boy, and as he was not sure how long he might be away, he wished to guard as far as possible against future complications.

He returned to the inn at Crowestoft village, and spent the evening going over his notes on the case.

Returning to town by the early morning train, he booked his passage by the Mauretania, and he sighed sorrowfully as he saw the number of his berth was that of the one Tinker had occupied when he crossed.

"Poor Tinker! What had become of him?"

He blamed himself for sending the lad on such a precarious

journey. But he had seemed so eager to go.

"We'll search the whole globe for him, old chap!" he said, addressing Pedro, who sat beside him.

•   •   •   •   •

Blake had an uneventful journey across, and they docked at noon five days later. He immediately proceeded to Mulberry Street, and found Carter at his desk.

"Well—well, this is a pleasant surprise!" exclaimed Carter, rising and grasping his hand cordially.

"I'm glad to see you again!" answered Blake, returning the grip.

"I suppose you have come over to look for the boy?" asked Carter, resuming his seat.

"Exactly," answered Blake, drawing up a chair. "I feel sure there has been foul play, and I blame myself for sending him alone."

"He seemed mighty bright," remarked Carter, "and appeared able to look after himself. Murphy, one of my men, took a great fancy to him, and was terribly cut up over his disappearance. He blames himself for it."

"Tell me what you know about it," said Blake. "I know nothing but what was in your cable."

Carter explained what had happened up till Murphy had got left on the Elevated station.

"Murphy, of course, wouldn't have any idea at which station they would get out," mused Blake, as Carter finished.

"No; but he went to every station below Forty-Second Street, and tried to pick up the trail. One of the cops on Fourteenth Street did tell him he saw two persons who fitted the description going east, one behind the other, but he lost the trail there.

"It's mighty hard for us to get any information now on the East Side," he added. "The cops there mostly stand in with the dens, and keep their eyes shut to a good deal that goes on. We can't, unfortunately, depend on them for assistance, as you can with your London police. Murphy has spent a good deal of time down there looking for the boy, but they know him pretty well by now, and he can't do much. It's pretty hard for him to disguise that Irish face of his," Carter laughed.

"I'd like to talk with him, if you don't mind," Blake said.

"Why, certainly! I'll see if he is in now." And Carter rang.

"Is Murphy in?" he asked, as the patrol man entered.

"Yes, sir; he came in a few moments ago."

"You might send him to me."

"Yes, sir." And the man, saluting, withdrew.

"Murphy, let me introduce you to a man you greatly admire—Mr. Sexton Blake," said Carter, as Murphy entered.

"I'm proud to meet you, sir," said Murphy, big eyes lighting with pleasure at the fulfilment of one of his dearest wishes.

"Murphy is always dinning your merits in my ears," laughed Carter. "I don't know where he gets the information, but he seems to know every case you are working on."

Murphy blushed to the roots of his hair with pleased embarrassment at Carter's remark as Blake shook hands, but the great detective soon put him at his ease.

"I wonder if you could spare me Murphy for a few days?" he said, turning to Carter; and Murphy's eyes lit up with eagerness as he awaited the reply.

"I guess I'll have to, Blake. If I refused, I wouldn't get any work out of him all the time you were here. But you will find him just the man you want," he added, "and you can depend on him absolutely."

"Truly, sir, it wasn't my fault that I missed the train that night," broke in Murphy. "I swore and nearly tore the place down, I was so mad." And from the expression in his eyes one could easily imagine that the officials at the Elevated station had experienced a warm half-hour.

"I won't take up any more of your time now," said Blake, rising. "I'll communicate with you frequently, and may ask for your assistance."

"I'll be only too pleased to do anything I can for you," answered Carter. "I'm working on the murdered Miller case now, but don't hesitate to ask me for any men you need."

"Thanks!" replied Blake. And the two greatest detectives in the world shook hands, Murphy being a highly-flattered spectator.

"I'll take you along with me now, Murphy, if you are ready," said Blake, picking up his hat.

"Yes, sir; I am quite ready." And Murphy saluted Carter and followed Blake.

"Where are we going first, sir?" asked Murphy, as they gained the street.

"I want first to go to the dock and get my dog, and then we will go up to the Belmont. I wish to look after poor Tinker's things." And his eyes grew grave as he spoke.

Murphy hailed a taxi, and they were soon threading their way through the traffic to the docks.

Pedro was delighted in a dignified manner at his liberation, and took an immediate liking to Murphy, which pleased the latter immensely. The great, intelligent beast sniffed the air deeply, as though he would wrest from it the secret of his young master's disappearance.

As they entered the Belmont, Blake sent for the manager, and as he conversed with him, Pedro was the disdainful recipient of much attention, to Murphy's grinning delight.

"Well, say, ain't he a stunner?" said one.

"I reckon he could give some of them Virginy dogs cards and spades and beat 'em," remarked another.

"He ain't takin' no dope from you," said a third, as Pedro took no notice of the attention he was receiving.

"Say, mister, how much do you want for him?" asked one of Murphy.

"Nix on that," replied Murphy. "He ain't mine. He belongs to my friend over there, and he wouldn't sell him for a million."

"Gee! He must have some stuff! Who is he?"

"Who is he? He's J. P. Morgan's long-lost brother." And Murphy chuckled at the astonished look on their faces.

Breaking away from their questions, he joined Blake, and with Pedro padding along beside them, they took the elevator and ascended to Blake's room, which was the same one the absent Tinker had engaged but had never slept in. Blake's eyes filled as he looked at the boy's bags on the floor, and he walked to the window, staring out to collect himself. Pedro gave a great bay of joy as he nosed the articles, but he turned great, sorrowful, inquiring eyes on Blake when the owner of them did not appear also. From, that moment the faithful animal seemed to realise that he was near his beloved friend, and he eyed everything and everybody that he came in contact with, as though he would find in them the answer that he wanted.

Blake turned from the window, and, taking the noble fellow's head in his hands, said:

"Have patience, old chap! We'll find him yet, if he's alive!" And Pedro pushed his wet nose deeper between his hands in trustful confidence.

Murphy's warm Irish heart ached at the sight, and he brushed a hand across his eyes.

"Now, Murphy," said Blake, rising, "I'm going to disguise you so that your own mother wouldn't know you."

"Bedad, I'm afraid it's impossible, Mr. Blake. Mr. Carter has tried me often, but they pick me every time on the east side."

"Never mind," laughed Blake. "I'll show you a new trick. You can't lose your accent, so you'll have to be Irish; but I'll fix you up so the sharpest 'tough' on the Bowery can't pick you." And, suiting the action to the word, he placed Murphy in a chair and went to work.

"Now take a look at yourself in the glass!" he said, as he finished. And Murphy walked to a mirror, where he stood gazing at himself in comical astonishment.

"Glorious Oireland! Is that me?" he ejaculated.

"It certainly was you," answered Blake; "but I must confess I'm rather pleased myself with the job. That scowl doesn't look much like you, and when I get you rigged up you'll look like the surliest Irish navvy that wielded a pick."

"Bedad, the bhoys of Mulberry Street wouldn't call me 'Irish' now if they saw this bee-utiful scowl you've given me." And his face assumed a terrifying expression as his grin, mixed with the made-up scowl.

"You mustn't indulge in any smiles," warned Blake; "you'd give yourself away at once, not counting the people you would send into hysterics with that contortion."

"I won't, I promise you. I'm too anxious to find the boy." he said soberly, "What are you making up as, sir?"

"I'm going to be a Bowery 'tough,' in funds and very flash," answered Blake, "and you are to be, presumably, on a drunk, and accompany me. You are to have been left a legacy, and I am to be getting the lot away from you. So you see you must pay for everything." And as he spoke he passed Murphy a large roll of American notes which he had got from the manager of the hotel.

An hour later there sallied forth from the back entrance of the Belmont, a drunken Irish navvy and a very flash Bowery "tough," accompanied by the wondering stare of the lounging bell-boys.

Pedro had been sent to Murphy's flat, to be taken care of by the latter's wife until they needed him.

53

THE TENTH CHAPTER.   Tinker on Board the Bertha — Hope Abandoned—Despair.

TINKER came to, conscious of a terrible pain in his head. He was in total darkness and could hear nothing but a gurgling sound. He tried to rise, but found himself bound hand and foot, and, sinking back, lapsed again into unconsciousness.

He awakened the second time, conscious of a pain in his leg, and, opening his eyes, became aware that a big, bearded man was kicking him into consciousness.

"'Ere, you bloomin' dog, wake up! You've had all the beauty sleep you'll get for some time."

"Where am I?" asked Tinker feebly.

"You get up and come along with me, an' you'll find out where you are," grinned the man evilly; and, leaning down, he cut Tinker's bonds and dragged him to his feet. The boy collapsed, and would have fallen, but the man held him, and roughly chafed his limbs, saying, as he did so: "You young fellers nowadays are soft as putty. When I was your age you could tie me in a knot an' lay me down on a bed o' spikes, an' I'd dream o' roses! Strike me pink, if I couldn't!"

As his limbs were being chafed, Tinker looked around, and became aware that the walls of his prison were sloping. He looked up, and saw that the dim light proceeded from an open hatch, and his heart sank as he realised he was in the hold of a ship and that he had been "shanghaied."

"Now, come along!" said the man roughly, and jerked him to a ladder which led out of the hold to the deck.

Tinker put a brave face on the matter and climbed up, his legs and fingers so stiff he could hardly make the journey. Reaching the deck, while he waited for his guide he looked around, and saw he was on a small, dirty tramp steamer.

"I suppose you know where you are now?" grunted his guide, emerging from the hold. "Come along, now, and see the captain!" he growled, and led the way along the filthy deck and up a rickety ladder to the caricature of a poop-deck. Opening a door, he entered, and pulled Tinker after him.

"'Ere's the beauty!" he said, as he got inside; and Tinker, looking up, saw that he addressed a stout, bearded man whose brutal face reminded him of the bar-keeper in the Bowery den. "I don't see what you bother with lightweights for." he continued.

"You mind your own bloomin' business, which is being mate of this ship and obeying orders!" came the reply, in a drunken attempt at authority from what was obviously the captain. "I got good mon—" But he checked himself, and his face got even redder than it was with sullen anger as he saw the mate had heard.

"Oh, you did get good money, did you? An' might I ask why you've been so bloomin' quiet about it? Your delicate feelings couldn't stand the mention of such a vulgar subject, I s'pose?" remarked the mate sarcastically.

"Don't you give me any of your cheek! I'll do as I bloomin' well please on my own ship."

"No, you won't; not with me!" answered the mate, with a curse. "I know too much, and—"

"Never mind, we'll talk later," interrupted the captain, recollecting Tinker's presence.

But Tinker's sharp wits had absorbed the remarks he had heard, and he wondered who had paid the captain to get him out of the way.

"Now, sonny," continued the captain, taking a pull at a bottle and addressing Tinker, "you're going on a nice two years' cruise, and if ye're a good boy, and do what ye're told, you'll be well treated." And he leered drunkenly. "But if you don't—well, they say Mr. Brown"— and he looked at the mate— "has a heavy hand, so take my advice and keep clear o' it." And he leered again.

Tinker wisely refrained from asking any questions, and being asked if he understood, he nodded, and was ordered to go.

"You go down to the fo'c'sle," said the mate, "and ask for Thompson. Say I sent you, and for him to keep you busy." And he slammed the door in Tinker's face, evidently to continue his arguing over the money with the drunken captain.

Tinker found his way to the fo'c'sle, and asked for Thompson. A red headed Scotsman answered to the name, and Tinker put him down as the least objectionable of the lot, resolving to cultivate his good will.

"Mr. Brown sent me down and told me to ask for you, and to tell you to give me something to do," said Tinker, as Thompson inquired what he wanted.

"All right, lad; sit down and eat something first. I'll give you some work after dinner."

Tinker took a tin plate, and going to the cook's galley got it filled with boiled salt beef and potatoes. He returned to the fo'c'sle, and, sitting on an upturned bucket, started to eat. Food had not passed his lips for many hours, and he was surprised how good the coarse fare tasted. As he ate he looked around, and, besides Thompson, saw four other men. Two he took to be Swedes, one—from his accent—an American, and the fourth was a big negro, with an ugly scar across his face.

They all seemed to take his presence for granted, and paid no attention to him. Consequently, he had a good opportunity to study them while he ate his food. He liked none of them, but the black least of all. Turning to Thompson, whom he found had a decent streak in him, he asked:

"Is this all the crew?"

"No, there is the engineer and another man; the nigger's also in the engine-room."

Tinker was glad of that, as he probably wouldn't come much into contact with him, and he had taken an intense dislike to him.

"Where are we heading for?" he asked Thompson.

"Well, I guess it won't do any harm to tell you, since we only stop at one port on the way, and the chances are you'll probably be well tied up there," answered the latter. "We're going around the Horn and up to Bering Straits for seals. We are what you call poachers," he laughed. "We'll be gone two years, so you will have a chance to get well acquainted before we get back."

Tinker shuddered at the thought of two years with these scoundrels; and vowed mentally to get away, if possible, at the port at which they intended to touch.

"Where do we stop at on the way?" he asked carelessly.

"Oh, you needn't put any hopes in that!" grinned the other. "You'll get no chance to get away there."

"If that is so why don't you tell me, then?" he asked quietly.

"Oh, I'll tell you! It's Vancouver; we stop there for supplies."

Tinker pondered the information as he finished his meal, and his thoughts turned to Blake.

He would be terribly worried, and would think he was dead. What a mess he had made of things! Blake would search the globe for him, though. And a lump rose in his throat as he pictured Blake and Pedro in the cosy room at Baker Street. "If only he could get a message to Blake! But it was probably out of the question to ask any of his shipmates, and, besides, he had no money to bribe them. Anyway, they would probably take the money first, and then tell the captain or the mate, and he would get into worse trouble than he already was. He would hope and watch his chance, and maybe something would turn up, and he would work hard and keep clear of the captain and the mate. With which sorrowful reflection he finished his meal and took his plate to the Chinese cook.

At that same moment Blake was reading Carter's cable telling of Tinker's disappearance.

The lad worked hard, and managed to escape with only an acquaintance with the mate's boot. They all seemed to think he had accepted his fate, except Thompson, who would turn a shrewd eye on Tinker as he sat in thought, and say:

"It ain't any use, youngster. You might as well give it up." And Tinker would flush at the surprising of his thoughts.

They had a pleasant trip through the tropics, and Tinker was young enough to forget his troubles for the time. But when he leaned over the rail at night and looked at the blazing gems of the tropical sky as the ship forged toward the brilliant Southern Cross, he would think of Blake and Pedro, and his eyes would be misty as he turned away to seek his rough bunk.

The steamer was a small one, and so old her rotten hulk rolled heavily in the smallest seas. They had a rough passage round the Horn, and Tinker never expected to see her survive. The captain was drunk almost continuously, and the mate ran things with a high hand. Thompson acted as bo'sun and second mate combined, and Tinker, having assiduously cultivated his good will, fared better than he expected.

The special Providence which seemed to watch over drunken men and rotten ships was evidently with them, for they got safely through the Straits, and laid their course for the north again.

Tinker spent many hours on that long journey figuring plans for escape, intending to put them into effect when the ship reached Vancouver, but as they entered the Sound he was taken by Thompson, bound securely, and locked in a dark inside cabin which had no window. He threw reserve to the winds, and pleaded hard with Thompson for a sporting chance. But Thompson said:

"I'm sorry, lad. I'd like to give you a sporting chance, as you ask, but I don't dare!" And as though afraid he might relent, he went away quickly, locking the door.

Tinker sank back upon the floor, full of despair and every hope gone.

THE ELEVENTH CHAPTER.   Saunders Returns from America—Goes to Alliston—Accepted as John Alliston—Jack is Suspicious.

WHILE Tinker was proceeding on his forced journey, and Blake was searching for him, the little village of Alliston was all agog with excitement, for the long-absent John Alliston had returned.

The news quickly flew from house to house, and he was universally voted a "fine gentleman."

"Hadn't he immediately visited the village, and hadn't he made great promises of future benefits for the villagers?"

Only one man, the old bookkeeper at the mills, seemed cold in his reception of the prodigal. His sight was failing, but his memory was good, and he was certain John Alliston's eyes had been "blue" when he went away.

However, he held his peace for the time, for he was old, and a new position would be hard to find, and as he stopped to listen to a conversation between the cobbler and the barber he knew his suspicions would be ridiculed.

"I remember 'im well," said old Simeon Gregg, the cobbler. "'E's changed a bit with the years, 'e 'as, but 'e's the same free-'earted feller he was when 'e was 'ere before."

And he shook his grey head in pleasant reminiscence.

"I see'd 'im when 'e come out o' Lawyer Frost's office," chimed in the barber, "and he went over to the pub, and bought all the boys a drink, as pleasant-like as could be."

"'Ow do you know?" asked the cobbler.

"Well, I happened to go right in after 'im, and saw."

"Trust you to be round where any free drinks was goin'." And the barber shifted at the blunt thrust.

"Any'ow, 'e's a fine gentleman," he said. "'E told us 'e was goin' to give us a big time at the 'all in honour of 'is 'ome-comin'. 'E's a fine' man, 'e is." And the barber licked his lips at the thought of the future enjoyment in store for him.

"'Is figure 'as changed a bit," remarked the cobbler. "I thought as 'ow 'e would fill up like 'is father, but 'e's grown stouter like."

"Yes, 'e must take a bit after his mother. I never see'd 'er—did you, Gregg?" asked the barber.

"Oh, I see'd 'er often. The fust time I remember was one day

59

when I was up at the 'all after some o' the servants' shoes. Young Jack was a little feller at the time, an' while I was there 'e 'ad an accident. 'E'd bin playin' wi' one o' 'is father's guns, an' it went off an' blew the little finger o' 'is left 'and inter the air. 'Is mother was mighty worried about it, an' I see'd 'er then for the fust time. She was a fine woman," he added reminiscently.

"I never knew 'ow that 'appened," remarked the barber, "but I remember seeing it on 'is 'and when 'e lifted 'is glass in the pub, yesterday."—And the two worthies continued their discussion of the great event.

At about the same time the newly returned John Alliston sat at ease in the comfortable library at the Hall, and the worthy villagers would have been astonished could they have looked in upon him, for the butler Harris lounged at his ease opposite him, smoking familiarly.

"Well, this is something like!" remarked Harris, stretching his legs to the fire. "You certainly are a wonder, Saunders!" he added, looking at his companion admiringly.

"Don't use that name, even when alone," replied the other. "It's too dangerous. Everything has passed off splendidly," he continued. "I spent some time in the village yesterday, and not one of them twigged; they all accepted me without a word. Of course, Alliston wasn't in the village much when he was here; and, besides, those who would know the difference are all dead, except the old bookkeeper at the mills. He did seem a bit cautious about it, but if the old bird gets suspicious he will meet with a regrettable accident, I'm afraid."

"The police haven't found out anything," Harris said reflectively. "But I'm nervous about that Sexton Blake. He's been down here twice since the murder, and I heard young Alliston say before he returned to school that he had put him on the case,"

"Why in thunder didn't you tell me that before!" snapped Saunders, sitting up with a jerk. "I never dreamed of that. It explains a lot I didn't understand. I'll bet it had some connection with my being shadowed in New York."

"Shadowed in New York!" exclaimed Harris in surprise. "Who shadowed you?"

"Some young fellow. I was walking over Forty-Fourth Street to Sixth Avenue, and saw him in a mirror walking behind me. I didn't think anything at the time; but when I noticed him in the Elevated again, and saw him get out and walk behind me to the Bowery, I knew I was being followed. I went in Bowery Pete's place and tipped Pete off, and slipped out the back way. Pete told me the next day that the youngster took the bait beautifully, and I had him ship the boy away to the sealing grounds. He won't come back from there in a hurry," he said grimly. "But he must have been acting for Sexton Blake," he added, "and if he was that means trouble. Blake will stick to the trail till the last gun-fire."

"He'll do that all right," said Harris. "I think we ought to make a move to find out what he is doing."

"If Blake gets too close to me, he'd better look out for himself!" answered Saunders. "I'll run up to London in a day or two and find out what I can. We can't risk anything now. My plans have worked out exactly as I laid them, and I won't have Sexton Blake's interference!" he added, and his eyes glittered as he spoke.

"How about young Alliston?" asked Harris.

"I have written to him and told him I have returned, and added I would run up to Crowestoft in a few days to see him. I want to get more familiar with the old man's papers before I risk that."

"You'll have to handle him easy," said the other. "He's all for finding his grandfather's murderer, and isn't interested in anything else."

"I'll please him there all right. I'm going to stir up the police into fresh activity, and do all I can to find the scoundrel," grinned Saunders. "But leave me now, Harris. This Blake matter worries me. The more I think of it the more positive I am that he is following some definite clue; and if that is the case, we'll have to deal with him quickly. He's worse than a bloodhound on a trail, and I must plan some move to meet him."

    •   •   •   •   •

Crowestoft School presented a very similar appearance on an afternoon a few days later as it did when Sexton Blake had made his last, visit there.

As the returned "John Alliston" swung across the quad., and rang the bell of the doctor's residence, he felt a glow of almost personal pride as he reflected that he was the acknowledged father of one of the pupils of the exclusive academy. He was admitted by the same trim maid who had admitted Blake, and shown in to await the doctor.

"Mr. Alliston, I presume?" said the doctor, smiling as he entered, and holding out his hand.

"Yes," replied his visitor. "I suppose you got my letter saying I was coming?" he inquired as they sat down.

"Yes; and sent for your son immediately. He had also received me, and is now waiting to be sent for."

"Ah! I will be glad to see the boy!" And Alliston affected the anxious father to perfection.

"I will send for him now," replied the doctor, ringing.

"You and I can talk later. You have been away a good many years, Mr. Alliston," he continued, as they waited for Jack.

"Yes; I acted as a good many others do when the blood is young I went away in anger, and although I intended to write, things went very hard with me for some years; but they turned later, and I waited, in foolish pride, until I could come home with a fortune. I will blame myself all my life for not writing before my father's shocking death; and what makes it harder, is, that I only missed seeing him by a few weeks. But I have stirred up the police, and will spend every penny I have, if necessary, to find his murderer," and his eyes flashed with just exactly the proper light.

Jack heard the last sentence as he knocked and opened the door, and his heart warmed instantly to the man who had spoken it. Alliston gained a bigger footing in a moment with Jack by that remark than he would otherwise have done by months of assiduous labour to gain the boy's good will.

"Quite right, I honour you for your remarks, Mr. Alliston," replied the doctor. "Come, Jack," he continued, "I know you are anxious to talk with your father, so I will leave you for a little." And he retired.

"Well, Jack, I have at last come home," said Alliston, beginning the conversation and breaking the silence which threatened to develop into an embarrassing situation.

"I'm glad to see you, sir!" answered Jack, coming forward and holding out his hand.

Alliston was not by any means the repellent type one would expect to find in a man who possessed the amount of evil in his nature which he did. He was rather attractive than otherwise, and as he stood there that afternoon, his big frame held erect and his face covered by a well-trimmed, fair beard he looked the well-travelled man of the world to the last detail. Jack was not to be blamed that, hungry as he was for a parent, he should fail to read below the surface. And, indeed, it needed a very clever man to read Mr. John Alliston. It was that fact that made him a dangerous, and up until then a successful criminal. He would do anything to gain his object, but he worked scientifically, and only a man of Sexton Blake's attainments would worry Alliston. For the police he cared not a fig.

"I was under the impression, sir, that grandfather said you had blue eyes," remarked Jack, after they had been chatting for some time.

Alliston cursed his luck in not knowing that point, but replied laughingly:

"Oh, no; they were rather blue when I was a child, but as I grew older they faded to a grey. I trust you are not suspicious of my identity, are you, Jack?" he added, smiling And Jack never knew how, under that smile, the pulse quickened with anxiety as he awaited the boy's answer.

"Oh, no. sir I only made the remark as a matter of course."

"I see, well, I must be going now, my boy. I want to catch the evening train to town, as I have several matters to attend to. I will run down in a few days to see you again, Jack, and you can come to town with me for a day or two."

"I trust, sir, you will do what you can to find grandfather's murderer." said the boy, as they arose. "I heard what you said as I entered."

"I will—I will, Jack! As I said, I will spend every penny I have, if necessary, to bring the scoundrel to justice."

"I'm so glad!" replied the boy. "He was very good to me. By the way, sir, I ought to tell you, I suppose, that Mr. Sexton Blake is working on the case for me."

"Ah!" replied Alliston. "has he found out anything yet?"

"No, sir, not yet; but he hopes to soon. He went to New York three weeks ago on business, but I haven't heard anything from him yet."

"He didn't give you any idea as to what took him there?" asked Alliston, calmly, but his mind was in a turmoil at the information he had just received.

"No; he didn't say. I hope you will see him when he returns sir."

"Yes, I will do so," replied Alliston. "Yes, I will positively see him immediately on his return," he added slowly.

THE TWELFTH CHAPTER. The Capture—Success for Saunders.

JOHN ALLISTON had made himself popular with the neighbourhood. He had given lavishly to charities, had raised the wages at the mills, had subscribed liberally to the hounds, and it was well known he was purchasing a string of hunters and polo-ponies that would delight the heart of any horseman. He was having extensive alterations made in the old house, and it was rumoured that when they were finished he would entertain extensively and give the Hall a mistress. His boyhood marriage was forgotten, and he was a welcome guest by every anxious mother with a marriageable daughter.

Life was, indeed, treating John Alliston well, and only one thought occurred to interrupt his pleasant musings as he sat in his library smoking a choice cigar and planning for the future. That thought was Sexton Blake. He had made several trips to London, and had set a man to watch for Blake's return from New York. He had instructed the man to wire him instantly on Blake's arrival, and then he would act. He knew without any doubt that Blake was a big element of danger, and that he must be suspicious of something. Alliston had gone over and over his movements, and could see no mistakes; but, still, he felt that in some way the famous detective had seized on a point.

His thoughts were interrupted by the entrance of Harris.

"There's a man at the door says he wants to see you. I said you were busy, but he said he would wait. I told him it wouldn't be any use, but he says it's important, and he must see you if he has to wait a week."

"What does he look like?" asked Alliston.

"He doesn't look unlike you, with that fair beard on. He's big, like you, too."

"I don't know who it can be," mused Alliston. "There is only one I know who fits that description, but it can't be he. No; that's impossible! It can't be so very important. Probably someone with a hunter to sell. Send him in, Harris," he said, "and remain near the door in case I should need you," and the cautious Alliston again proved his cleverness.

"All right; I'll fetch him along," said Harris, leaving.

A few moments later a big, fair-bearded man pushed aside the curtains over the door and entered.

"My heavens!" gasped Alliston. "You!" And he stared at the man as though he were a ghost.

"Yes; it is I! And although you are well disguised, I know you as well," he replied, in a steely voice. "I heard in the village of the return of John Alliston, and wondered who had usurped my name and position. I came to see, and now I know. You are changed, but I'll always remember your eyes, Jim Carson. Heaven only knows how many other names you've got! I know, now, who killed the faro-dealer and stole my papers telling who I really was. I also know who realised on the claim I found. Oh, you were very clever! It took nerve, but you knew no one else but the dealer looked at the plan of the claim, and only I, besides, knew where it was. You played the drunkard very well, but I now know the meaning of your smile in the court-room. I suppose you dissipated the money you made from the claim, and, by the use of the information gained from my private papers, now hope to get the Alliston estates by posing as me? No doubt the murder of my father was the first step in the game, and Heaven knows what other plans you have conceived. For the ten years of torture you gave me I am going to thrash you within an inch of your life, and the law can then deal with you for the murder of my father." And though he spoke with a deadly calm, his breast heaved with suppressed emotion.

Saunders was not a coward, and was every bit as powerful as the other man, but he saw a deadly purpose in his eyes, and he knew it would be a fight to the death between them— he knew it must be settled there and then. His mind worked like lightning, and he decided his only chance was to be the aggressor instead of the attacked. He would have to try a bluff first.

"You must be either mad or deluded," he said suavely, getting to his feet carelessly. "I am John Alliston, and I don't understand your remarks."

"You liar! How long do you think you can bluff a story like that with me, the rightful John Alliston, here, besides, you will never have the chance, for I'm going to kill you here and now."

And Alliston moved towards him menacingly.

Saunders saw he could stave off the attack no longer, and, cursing himself inwardly for being without his revolver, and with the one cry "Harris!" he sprang like a tiger at the other.

Alliston had never dreamed Saunders would lead up the attack, and he was unprepared for the sudden spring; but as he felt the grip of the other man's fingers on his throat, he brought his left hand up under Saunders' arms until it reached his chin, while his right reached around to the small of his opponent's back. Saunders' body grew tense to resist the pressure, and the two straining giants struggled in rapid circles round the room. Chairs were knocked over, and furniture smashed as they struggled for the mastery. Harris entered, and, seeing the struggle, rushed to the fireplace and seized a heavy poker; he stood watching his chance to strike Alliston, but the fight waxed too hot, and the struggling men were shifting so rapidly, he didn't dare bring it down, for fear of hitting Saunders.

Saunders had secured a strong hold on Alliston's throat, and the pressure of his powerful hands was making itself felt, but Alliston's hand was pushing back his head with an unyielding force, while the pressure of his arm in the vital part of Saunders' back was causing him excruciating pain. Saunders made a supreme effort to sink his fingers further in his opponent's throat, for he realised that if his chin gave an inch, the awful pressure would break his neck like a pipe-stem; but Alliston's throat yielded not an atom, and Saunders' eyes filled with horror as he felt his chin yielding to the terrible strain. He knew he was failing, and that it meant his sudden death, and he didn't want to die.

They had stopped whirling in the struggle, and each was straining with a last-effort—one must give way soon. No human frame could withstand the tremendous pressure that each was exerting. Saunders felt his chin going back, back another half-inch would put it past the balance point, and he knew it would fly back sharply when that point was reached. With a gasping whisper of "Harris!" he yielded to the pressure, and dropped, but that momentary stop in the fight had saved his life, for Harris had seized the opportunity presented, and, as Saunders lost his hold, he brought the heavy poker down with crushing force on Alliston's head, and he dropped like a stone.

Saunders came to himself with a gasp as Harris forced some brandy between his lips. He fingered his neck gingerly as he sat up; it felt as though a cart-wheel had gone over it, and his back was giving him intense pain; but as he saw the senseless form of Alliston on the floor, he forgot his hurts in his satisfaction at the sight.

"He nearly got me that time," he said, getting up and going over to the body. "You saved my life all right, Harris, and I'll not forget it."

"I tried to get in at him several times." replied Harris. "But you were whirling round so fast, I didn't dare, for fear of cracking you instead."

"Well, you got him just in time; another second, and my neck would have gone with a crack. I don't ever want to feel the rope around it after that experience," he added, with a shudder at the thought.

"What are you going to do with him?" asked Harris.

"It would be too risky to kill him here. He'll come round in a little while, so we'll tie his hands and feet. The best plan will be to lock him in that lumber-room in the garret until we get a chance to run him through to the coast. I'm having the old Alliston yacht refitted, and it will be ready for sea next week. We'll keep him until then, and take him in the motor to a quiet cove. I'll have the yacht brought around, and we can take him aboard at night. It will be easy to weight his body and drop it over out at sea a bit."

"That will be by far the safest plan," replied Harris. "It won't do to create any suspicions down here now when things are going so well. I will go and get James to bring some rope, and we'll truss him up. If he does yell, no one can hear him from that room."

James had been promoted from the work which he hated, and was enjoying himself lording it over a number of stablemen when Harris found him. He got some strong rope, and between them they trussed up Alliston. They carried him to the room in the garret where they deposited him roughly in a corner. His senses had not yet returned, and they left him to come round himself.

The pseudo Alliston dined at Lord Raymonde's that night, and made himself particularly agreeable to the Honourable Violet, Lord Raymonde's daughter.

THE THIRTEENTH CHAPTER.   Blake as the Count — Bowery Pete's on a Busy Night—The Fight.

THE evening was at its height in Bowery Pete's den. The bar was lined with drinking toughs, and the tables were occupied by a larger number than usual of women with attendant drunken swains. The lowest type of all nationalities were represented there that night. A big Swedish sailor shed maudlin tears on a negro's neck, a Spaniard clinked glasses with a ponderous German, a Russian forgot hereditary differences in singing a duet with a Pole, while a number of English, Scotch and American seamen made the atmosphere blue with their profane conversation. The men in tow of the harpies' tables were mostly sailors of every nationality.

It was election night in New York, and Tammany Hall had gained the day. That meant the undisturbed operation of the gambling and drinking dens, and the East Side accordingly rejoiced. The noise waxed fast and furious, and an extra man behind the bar hovered near the switch of the electric lights to be ready to turn them out if a fight should start—and there would be several there that night.

Before the lights were turned out, the regular habitues of the place would pick their man. While he staggered in the dark, they would get to him with the butt end of a revolver, and he would drop. The trick was worked scientifically, and the victims would find themselves thrown out on the street, stripped of what money they possessed. Some few who knew no better would complain to the police, but they never did so a second time. If the fight was too severe for the hangers-on to deal with, guns were brought into play, and a shrill whistle fetched the police. The victims were hustled out, and three months in Blackwell's Island Prison taught them the futility of complaining against the scientific organisation of "graft," which stretched from the high ranks of the police to the most insignificant Bowery "tough." Pete paid his contributions every month, for which he expected a free hand, and he got it.

On the particular night in question, the pandemonium had reached the height where a fight was imminent, when the door opened, and a typical Bowery "speiler" lurched down the steps which led from the street. He was evidently well known to some of the habitues, for he was greeted familiarly on all sides as the "Count."

He was dressed in the most flashy style, as approved by the

Bowery. Conspicuous check suit, patent-leather shoes with grey tops, a pink shirt and pinker tie, with a round soft felt hat resting on one side of his head, and pulled down over one eye, made up his appearance, he wore a huge, flashing "phony " diamond in his tie, and a cigarette stuck at an angle in his mouth; his hands were thrust into the side pockets of his coat, and he lurched about with a swaggering bravado. Such was the Count, and one could certainly see in the flashy tough who entered, no resemblance to the famous detective, Sexton Blake; but he it was.

The Count was evidently in an expensive mood that evening, for he pushed his way through the crowd which argued in front of the bar, and told Pete to serve everyone. Pete served the least drunk with a medium drink, the half drunk with flavoured water, and the very drunk with nothing at all, but collected from the Count for the lot. The Count made no demur, for it was an understood thing that a drink for the crowd was served at Pete's discretion with payment for all.

The Count tossed down his own drink, and his glance roved around the reeling mass, resting for just a fraction of a second on a man in the far corner. Turning to the bar, he leaned over and talked casually with Pete. He swung round after a few moments, and made his way in a circuitous manner past the tables, stopping occasionally for a word with a man, or to answer the sally of a leering woman. He gradually drew nearer to the corner, and as he reached the table next to that at which the object of his glance sat, he pulled out a chair, and ordered a drink from a murderous-looking waiter.

Blake had spent many weary weeks leading the life of a Bowery tough, spending his days and nights in their haunts. He had visited them all in the role he adopted, but found that while he had Murphy with him as a "good thing," although his perfect impersonation had made him accepted as genuine, they respected his game. Friendly though he had been able to get, he had consequently not achieved the intimacy he desired; he had therefore decided to leave Murphy outside, where he could reach him if he needed him, and start the rounds of the dens alone. He picked on Bowery Pete's first, as it was the headquarters of the cleverest speilers, and those were the ones with whom he wished to get in touch, for they had a thorough knowledge of all the happenings in the great underworld of the East Side.

He had recognised the man in the corner as one of the cleverest of the lot, a man called the "Kid," and he resolved to place himself so the Kid would open up a conversation.

The pushing back of a chair told him his neighbour was getting up, and he puffed on calmly, as he waited to see if the Kid would make any advance.

"Are you waiting for anyone?" asked a voice; and; looking up, he saw the Kid standing beside him.

"No, just thinking out a plan. Sit down, will you?"

"Sure thing," replied the Kid.

"Quite a crowd of strange ones here to-night," remarked Blake, beckoning to the waiter, and ordering two more drinks.

"Yes, there'll be rough house soon, I reckon. What became of that Irish 'mark' you had, Count? Did you get all he had?"

"Yes, I stripped him quick; he was an easy mug," replied Blake.

"You haven't been around very long, have you?" asked the Kid.

"Oh, I've been here before, but I took a few years' vacation up the river." (Sing Sing Prison.)

"You would have been around before my time, then," remarked the Kid. "I've only been round a couple of years. By jiminy! There'll be a rumpus soon," he added, glancing at the crowd around the bar, who were getting noisier every minute.

"Yes, it looks like it. I'll sit right here, I think, if the light goes. I'm not particular about a mix-up to-night," said Blake.

"Got something on?" inquired the Kid, laughing.

"Yes, a 'good thing,'" answered Blake, laughing also.

"That big nigger will be going through the trap if he gets much noisier," broke in the Kid, as their attention was attracted by a particularly loud argument at the bar.

"I didn't know Pete worked that game much now," remarked Blake carelessly.

"He hasn't lately, but after to-day's election it will be safer. He has only worked it for big money the past two years."

"I got hold of a cinch a few weeks ago," said Blake. "He was a young buck, and had a good roll on him. I made an appointment with him one night, but he never turned up, and I haven't seen him since. I often wondered if he was 'dropped' any place, or if he got wise and cleared out," and he laughed. "He had plenty of gilt, and I hated to lose him, as I needed it at the time," he added.

"Pete dropped a young fool here not long ago," remarked the

Kid. "It was a special job, though, and he probably wasn't your mug."

"I suppose not," replied Blake. "What did they do with him, the usual?" he asked casually.

"Yes," replied the Kid. "Shipped him on the Bertha to the Arctic."

"I'm sorry if it was my man," laughed Blake. "I would have liked to have got his money first."

"I like your cut, Count," said the Kid, changing the subject. "I wonder why we couldn't work in together?"

"No reason in the world why we couldn't," replied Blake. "Have you anything good on?" he added.

"Yes; and I'll let you in on it if you'll split on yours."

"That's a go," answered Blake. "Let's hear what yours is."

"Well, it's this way." And the Kid leaned over, speaking low. "Old Ryan, up at Tammany, says that—"

But just then the noise at the bar reached the climax, and the place was plunged in darkness.

Blake and the Kid both rose to their feet, while from all around them came a pandemonium of yells, shrieks, curses, groans, and thuds as bodies fell to the floor.

"Stick close to me, and we'll make for the door," said the Kid. And Blake drew his gun, following close.

The Kid seemed to know his way thoroughly in the dark, for he worked his way confidently through the struggling mass. They had got about halfway to the door when a revolver shot rang out, and then another, and another, and soon over half of the drunken fighters were shooting indiscriminately in the dark. Their reason was running amok, and Blake realised the police would soon be there if it kept on. A groan beside him, and the Kid dropped. Blake bent down to help him, but as he did so a panic-stricken mob of drink-crazy men and women swept over the room, seeking the door, screaming with hysterical laughter and curses, and carrying Blake in its midst. Men were hitting anywhere in the dark, and Blake, turning his revolver around, hit out with the butt-end and cleared a circle.

It was pitch-dark, and he had lost his bearings in the melee. He groped his way around until he found the wall. A bullet whizzing past his ear buried itself close to him, and the shooting started again. Dropping to his knees he followed the wall, and was fortunate enough to find the steps leading to the street. Hastily getting to his feet, he made his way out, and drank in the fresh air in deep breaths.

"Heavens! What a hole!" he muttered, straightening his clothes. "But it was worth it. I've got what I want, and now to act."

Half a dozen police appeared around the corner on the run, and Blake, lighting a cigarette, strolled carelessly up the street.

THE FOURTEENTH CHAPTER.   Off to Vancouver—Pedro Takes a Hand—Tinker Rescued.

BLAKE picked up Murphy at the next corner, and together they proceeded to the Belmont.

"I heard the shots," said Murphy, "and was coming to your assistance when I saw you appear; then, seeing the police, I stopped. Did you find out anything, Mr. Blake?"

"Yes. I had about given up hope, Mr. Murphy, but I pumped the one they call the Kid, and he told me what I wanted to know. He was shot in the row, so I didn't get the information any too soon."

"I'm right glad, sir," said Murphy. "I hope they haven't killed the lad," he added anxiously.

"No; I think he will be alive yet, but we've got to reach him quick."

"Where is he, sir?"

"They 'shanghaied' him in Pete's, and shipped him on a boat called the Bertha to the Arctic. That's all I know so far. I want you to slip around and ask Carter for unlimited leave. I will go on to the Belmont, and find out where the ship is headed for."

"All right, sir; I won't be long." And Murphy hurried away.

Blake hailed a taxi and went to the Belmont, where he changed and went to the office. He looked up the Bertha in the shipping list, and found the information he wanted. Several telegrams were waiting for him, and the sending office marked on them was Reno Nevada. Blake smiled in satisfaction as he read them.

"As I thought," he muttered, as he seated himself and waited Murphy's return.

"Did you find out about the Bertha?" asked Murphy, as he entered.

"Yes; and the list says she has sailed for Vancouver by the Horn in ballast. I find, on looking up the dates, that we can just about make Vancouver as she gets there. I have sent up to have my bags packed, and we will catch the Montreal express."

"Good, Sir, I'll be glad to get my hands on the scoundrels who have got him!" added Murphy, and he clenched his great hands.

"You slip around to your flat and say good-bye to your wife," said Blake. "Bring Pedro, and meet me at the Grand Central Station in half an hour." And Murphy departed.

An hour later they were in the pullman of the Montreal Express, on what was to be an exciting trip.

•   •   •   •   •

"She's a dirty-looking tub."

It was Murphy who spoke, and he addressed Blake, who stood beside him.

They were standing in the shelter of a shed, watching a dirty grey steamer come into dock.

"Yes; if the vessel looks anything like the crew, they must be a choice lot," answered Blake. "We'll go back to the hotel and wait until dark."

They turned, and threaded their way through the crowded bales up the dock.

They dined lightly, neither of them feeling inclined to eat much. Blake was pondering deeply, and Murphy was full of thoughts which boiled to audible curses when he dwelt on Tinker's plight.

After dinner Blake released Pedro, and it was a quietly determined trio that returned to the docks. They took up their position in a dark corner, and watched the ship for over an hour.

Blake was of the opinion that some of the crew would go ashore, and he was right. As eight bells struck around the harbour, four men left the ship and rolled up the dock. They waited until the quartette had disappeared at the head of the wharf, and then they silently moved over towards the ship, keeping under cover of some freight cars which stood near.

Pedro seemed conscious that important things were happening, for he sniffed the air suspiciously, and kept close to Blake. They succeeded in gaining the side of the steamer without being seen. Blake, lifting himself on to a bale, discerned a solitary man on watch, and in the dusk saw it was a negro. He got down noiselessly, and, beckoning to Murphy, the trio ascended the gangway.

Blake stepped quietly over the deck, and as he got near, the negro heard him, and turned. He opened his mouth to give the alarm, but Blake's fingers closed on his throat, choking the cry into a gurgle, and they grappled.

There was no time to waste, and Blake put all his strength into the pressure of his hands. The negro's grip of Blake relaxed, his eyes rolled, and he sank quietly to the deck. Not a word had been uttered, nor a sound made, and Murphy looked at Blake with undisguised admiration.

They moved silently across the deck, and ascended the poop deck. Listening at the companion-way, they heard voices below.

"We've no time to lose," whispered Blake; "the others may come back any moment, so we'll have to take our chances. Pull your revolver, but don't shoot unless you have to. The boy is here, I'll guarantee, and we'll probably have a fight to get him. Follow me."

And he sprang down the companion-way, with Murphy and Pedro after him.

As they reached the bottom, they found themselves in a small, dirty saloon. A table was screwed to the floor in the centre, around which three men were sitting, who proved afterwards to be the mate, Thompson, and the engineer. They looked up in consternation as the strange trio entered.

"Is either of you the captain?" asked Blake abruptly.

"No, he's not here," was the reply; "but I'm the mate, and might I ask what you mean by coming down here without an invitation? I'll wring that nigger's neck for letting you pass."

"It won't be necessary," replied Blake coolly. "I've already saved you the trouble. As for why we came here without an invitation, I'll tell you. We want the boy you shanghaied in New York."

"Wot boy? We ain't got no boy. And wot do yer mean by sayin' we 'shanghaied' anyone? You get out, and mind yer own bloomin' business."

"Look here, you might as well stop bluffing and blustering," said Blake. "If you haven't got the boy, why, all right, we'll leave. But I'm going to search first."

"Oh, you are, are you? Well, just let me see yer try. You get out quick, or I'll 'ave yer thrown out!"

While the altercation between Blake and the mate had been taking place, Murphy had been standing ready; but Pedro had disappeared. As Blake started to reply, a deep bay came from a dark alleyway which ran off the saloon, and a furious scratching sound followed. A faint voice floated to them, and Blake stopped to listen.

"Guv'nor! Guv'nor! I'm here! Help me, guv'nor!"

"All right, Tinker!" called Blake, while a guilty silence fell on the three at the table. "There is your answer," said Blake, as Pedro came bounding back into the saloon. "Are you going to deliver up the boy quietly, or have we got to take him forcibly?"

"I ain't goin' to deliver Jim up, and wot's more, you ain't goin' to take 'im!" And as he spoke, the mate jumped to his feet. "Come on and 'elp me put these interfering fools out!" he called to the other two, and sprang for Blake.

Blake was prepared for him, and they grappled, rolling over and over in the struggle. The mate was a powerful man, and much bigger than Blake, but the latter was lithe, and his muscles were like steel. They brought up against the table, and fought soundly.

The other two made for Murphy, who felled the engineer with one blow clean on the point of the chin. He and Thompson then sparred for holds, and the latter, rushing in, grappled. As they strained for the advantage, one of the Swedes and the nigger, who had evidently regained his senses, rushed down the companion-way. They grasped the situation, and while the Swede went to Thompson's assistance, the black went for Blake.

Pedro had been greatly excited while the fight proceeded, not knowing exactly what to do; but as he saw the negro make for Blake, his jaws opened, and, springing straight, he sank his teeth in the black's throat. Murphy was having a hard time. He had put Thompson to the floor, and was choking him into insensibility, when the big Swede landed on his back, and the three rolled over in a tangle of legs and arms.

Meanwhile, Blake, saved from extra odds by Pedro, had overcome the mate, who lay still. Calling Pedro off the negro, who also lay quiet in a pool of blood, he jumped for the others, and grappled with the Swede. Murphy, relieved of the Swede's attention, soon had the already half-beaten Thompson under control, and, dispatching him, he rose to his feet.

The Swede had Blake on his back. One hand was on his throat, and the other raised to descend with crushing force between the eyes, when Murphy, with a bellow of rage, jumped for him.

"Ye blonde-headed spalpeen!" he spluttered, returning to his native brogue in the excitement of the moment, and with the words he picked up the Swede, with an almost superhuman strength, and dashed him into the corner, where he lay motionless.

Helping Blake to his feet, they hastened down the alley, and Pedro stopped before a door, at which he scratched.

"We're coming, Tinker!" called Blake.

"All right, guv'nor. Hurry!" And at the voice Pedro nearly went mad with delight.

Stepping back, they made a combined rush at the door. Its rotten lock burst easier than they expected, sending them head over heels into the cabin.

It was pitch dark inside; but Murphy struck a match, and they saw Tinker lying bound in a bunk against the wall. They lifted him up and carried him out into the saloon, and tears of thankfulness filled Blake's eyes as they unbound him.

Tinker staggered to his feet, and they gripped hands silently; while Pedro rose and put his great paws on the lad's shoulders. Tinker then shook hands with Murphy, whose eyes were wet; and Blake said:

"We'll get out of this before any more come. We can talk at the hotel." And the joyful quartette hastened up the companion-way and over the side to the dock.

When they arrived at the hotel they had a sumptuous supper to celebrate the event, and Pedro actually threw his dignity to the winds in the enjoyment of it. Murphy sang "The Bowery, the Bowery, We'll never go there any more," after which they broke up and retired, as Tinker needed rest, and they were to leave on the morning express for Montreal.

Tinker told them his adventures on the journey east, and they landed at Montreal a week later. Murphy parted from them there, with tears in his honest eyes; but Blake told him, if Carter would spare him, he would use him in London. And Tinker knew, from the expression on Murphy's face as Blake spoke, that he would see Carter did spare him.

Blake, Tinker, and Pedro caught the Empress of Britain, and landed at Liverpool the following week, catching the first train on to Baker Street.

THE FIFTEENTH CHAPTER.   Saunders Gets Busy—Blake
Scores—The Inspector asks Help—Off to Alliston.

"WE can make a move soon now, Harris," remarked "Alliston," as he sat before his desk at Alliston with an open telegram in his hand. "Blake has arrived with a boy and a dog. I'd give a good deal to know if he has succeeded in getting that brat I sent to the Arctic. It beats me how he could."

"He might have picked up a boy in America to train," put in Harris.

"Yes, that's possible. Anyway, we've got to move at once."

"I won't be sorry," said Harris. "It's eight days now since we caught Alliston, and he's no joke to handle."

"Well, I'll write Blake to-night, and see if I can land him. The yacht will be ready in two days, and if Blake turns up, we can motor the pair of them over and get rid of them at once. I suppose I ought to run up to London and have a look at that boy, to see if it is the one who followed me in New York. But, pshaw! it's impossible. They wouldn't let him get away."

"What are you going to write him?" asked Harris.

"Oh, just a short note, saying I want him to come down and chat over the murder case with me." And he picked up his pen as he spoke and wrote.

•   •   •   •

"Well, I must confess that Mr. John Alliston has a colossal nerve." Blake made the remark to Tinker at breakfast, as he read a letter which he held in his hand.

"Who is John Alliston, guv'nor? Is he the Jack of whom you spoke?"

"No; he appears to be Jack's father, who has returned from abroad." And Blake smiled grimly as he spoke.

"He wasn't here before you left, was he?"

"No. He has apparently come back while we were in America. It's no use my seeing young Alliston now, until the matter ends one way or the other," he mused, "as he has already seen the boy."

"What is in the letter, guv'nor?" mumbled Tinker, his mouth full of marmalade and toast.

"I'll read it to you," replied Blake. "Just listen to this: "Dear Mr. Blake,—You will doubtless be surprised to receive a letter from me.

78

"'I arrived from abroad a few weeks ago, and my son Jack informs me that you are handling the case regarding the murder of my late father, and as I strongly desire to discover his murderer, I will be pleased to have you run down as my guest for a day, and while you are here we can discuss the matter.

"'Naturally, I am very anxious to clear up the matter as soon as possible, and bring to justice the scoundrel who committed the deed. And I must confess the police haven't done much so far.

"'Trusting you will be able to arrange to come, and awaiting your notification to that effect—I am, sir, yours, etc.

JOHN ALLISTON.' "

"What strikes you about that letter?" asked Blake, as he finished reading it.

"I don't know." replied the boy. "Seems keen on running down the murderer."

"I would like to know how he knew I had returned home. If he hadn't been watching for my arrival he would have written this before, and let it lay here until I came back. But it was written after we arrived at Baker Street. The trail grows hot, 'Mr. Alliston.' " And Blake rose.

"What are you going to do, guv'nor? Are you going down?"

"Yes, I'm going down. But not as 'Mr. Alliston's' guest. I'm travelling in a different way, and I want you to come."

"Do we take Pedro, guv'nor?"

"Oh, I think we can manage to keep him out of sight, if necessary!" laughed Blake. "He's as good as a man, and better than some," he added, pulling Pedro's ears, who, quite aware that he was the subject of the conversation, looked into Blake's eyes as he spoke.

"Are you going to answer Mr. Alliston's letter?" asked Tinker.

"Yes. I will write him now," answered Blake.

"Would you like to hear it, Tinker?'' he asked as he finished.

"Please, guv'nor."

"Well, listen, and I'll read it to you."

" 'Dear Mr. Alliston,—I am in receipt of your very kind invitation, and also note what you say about the case which I took for Master Jack.

"'I regret that I will be unable to visit you at present, as I am very busy, but hope to be able to meet you soon. I might say that I have nothing new to report on the case, but will resume the investigation shortly.

"'You will hear from me at once as soon as I make a move, and in the meantime I would advise patience.

"'Assuring you of my regret that I cannot accept your kind invitation, and that I have no progress to report to you at present—I am, sir, yours, etc., SEXTON BLAKE.'"

"You seem to have written a lot, guv'nor, and said nothing," remarked Tinker.

"That is just what I intended to do," replied the great detective. "And now, Tinker, 'phone for the car and pack the bags, and we will get ready to start for Alliston. We may be gone for some days."

"Is the Alliston affair really coming to a head, guv'nor?"

"Yes, very soon now. I will tell you more about it as we drive down."

Tinker telephoned for the car, and fifteen minutes later the big grey machine was standing at the door ready for the trip.

As they were preparing to leave Inspector Thomas was announced.

"Are you just going out, Mr. Blake?" he asked as he entered.

"Yes. Tinker and I are taking a run into the country," replied Blake. "But I can spare you a few moments. Did you wish to see me importantly?"

"Well, I did in a way. I must confess, Mr. Blake, that the Alliston murder has got me clean stumped, and I came round to see if you could give me any points." The inspector's pompous manner had all vanished, and he sat in a dejected manner, looking at Blake as though to read his thoughts.

"You ought to know more than I do, inspector. I have been in America for some weeks, and you have had the field to yourself."

"I know. I came round several times while you were away. I've been wondering if you've noticed anything I hadn't. I went down to see the son, who has just returned," continued the inspector. "I was suspicions of him at first, but on looking up the date he arrived in England, I found it was weeks after the murder. Besides, he's dead anxious to catch the murderer. He's been giving us no end of a time over it. Says a six-year-old child could fool us."

Blake smiled at the inspector's remarks.

"Oh, you can smile, Mr. Blake, but I assure you it's no joke to me! The chief has dragged me over the coals, and says if I don't show something soon he'll reduce me."

"I'm sorry to hear that, inspector, but I'll tell you what I'll do. You be patient for a few days, and when you get a telegram from me, come at once to wherever I say, and I'll hand you over the man who murdered Charles Alliston."

"You're joking, Mr. Blake!" said the inspector, staring in amazement at the detective.

"I never joke about such things," replied Blake, "and you know me well enough to know that I don't make a promise I can't fulfil, so if you do as I say, you can take the glory, and get back into the good graces of the chief."

"Oh, thank you, Mr. Blake! I'll be ready to come as soon as you telegraph to me."

"Oh, that's all right! We'll keep this little affair behveen ourselves, inspector," he added kindly. "Tinker won't say anything, and Pedro can't."

"I'm sure I'll be very grateful to you, Mr. Blake." said the inspector as he rose to go. "I won't forget it, I promise you." And he left with his mind at ease, for he knew the great detective would keep his word.

The inspector wasn't to be blamed for riding on Blake's horse, for he had a wife and family, and his position meant a living or starvation to him.

Blake shook his head and smiled as the inspector departed.

"I'm afraid, inspector," he said to himself, "when we meet on another case you'll be just as pompous and jealous as in the past. But there, it doesn't matter. Come along, Tinker, we'll get started." And they descended the stairs to the waiting machine.

Blake explained the case to Tinker as they drove along, and showed him how he arrived at his deduction.

"And you think he is the man, guv'nor?" asked Tinker as the detective finished.

"I know he is, Tinker, but I want him to make a certain move before I arrest him, which I'm sure he will," replied Blake quietly.

Two hours later they arrived at Alliston village and drove into the inn yard. Blake was travelling as Mr. Gates, and Tinker was his son. None of the villagers recognised in the driver of the great grey car, the simple-looking mechanic who had twice stayed at the inn.

THE SIXTEENTH CHAPTER.   The Chase to Liverpool—
Saunders Confident—Trail Grows Hot.

"I'M getting too suspicious in my old age," remarked Alliston to himself, as he leaned back in his chair, after reading Sexton Blake's letter. "I'm as nervous as an old woman, this man Blake is over-rated. He's no better than the police. I've certainly been a fool to worry over him as I have "—and he heaved a sigh of satisfaction. "He evidently doesn't suspect a thing; and it's too late for him to pick up the trail now. I'll write and tell him to come down whenever he can to discuss the case. His going to America got me worked up, but it must have been a pure coincidence. I'll feel safer to go ahead now, but I must get Alliston out of the way first. Why the devil couldn't he stay in prison? I'll just get Harris and arrange things." And suiting the action to the thought, he rang for the butler.

"This Sexton Blake bogey was all a myth." he remarked, as that worthy entered.

"How's that?" asked Harris.

"Read this letter, and you will see." answered Alliston, passing it over.

"H'm! Does look as though we've been scaring ourselves over him. But how do you explain his trip to America?"

"Pure coincidence, nothing else."

"This makes things much less complicated," remarked Harris.

"Yes, it would have been risky putting him out of the way, but no one knows the other exists, so he can be settled easily."

"When are you going to shift him?" asked Harris.

"I'll run down to Liverpool to-day, and see the captain of the yacht. I'll tell him to shift around to Bilton Cove— the place we picked on, you know—and we can take him down in a day or two."

"When will you be back?"

"I'll come back to-morrow, and we can probably arrange to do the job the following night."

"Right! Will I get James to drive you into the village?"

"Yes, and just pack a small bag for me."

As Harris went to carry out his instructions, Alliston leaned back and lit a cigar. From the smile on his face his thoughts must have been rather pleasant.

    •   •   •   •   •

"Quick, Tinker, get ready! We've got a race on!" said Blake, hurrying into their rooms at the inn.

"How do you mean?" asked Tinker, jumping up.

"Our man has just taken the train. I found out he had bought a return to Liverpool. I couldn't catch the train, so we'll have to race it in the car."

"All right, guv'nor, I'm ready now," said Tinker, and they were soon speeding along at a tearing pace for Liverpool.

"What do you suppose he has gone to Liverpool for?" asked Tinker.

"I don't know; but at the present stage of the game, I don't want to lose track of him for a moment."

"D'you think he's got suspicious, and is getting out of the country?"

"No, that occurred to me, but on my way to the inn I went in and saw the manager of the bank. He has drawn nothing from his account, and on the contrary, he paid in a large sum this morning."

"Maybe he's just taking a little jaunt," said Tinker.

"Possibly; but I don't want to lose sight of him."

They made rapid time to Liverpool, and drove to the railway station. Tinker jumped out and found the train wouldn't arrive for another seven minutes.

"We made great time," he said, climbing back into the car, but Blake was deep in thought.

"Take the car round to the Grand, Tinker, and wait for me there," said Blake arousing himself. "I don't know when I'll get back; but don't go away on any account until you hear from me. Alliston has never seen me, and I'm going to track him."

"All right, guv'nor! I'll wait for you!" And as Blake clambered out, Tinker started the car, and swung round to get to the Grand.

The detective only had a few moments at his disposal, and, entering the station, he made what was probably the quickest change in his career. As he walked down the platform he saw a large truck piled high with luggage awaiting the departure of a train. No one stood near it at the moment, and, hastening his footsteps, he walked behind it. He had to be quick, for someone might stroll along at any minute.

Taking off his coat, he turned it with lightning-like rapidity. The neat blue trousers were sprinkled with a harmless dust, and when the bottoms were turned up, they had the appearance of a well-worn pair of working trousers. The same powder rubbed on the boots gave them an old look, and the neat felt hat disappeared to be replaced by a seedy cap. A soiled neckerchief to replace the immaculate collar, and a short, blackened clay pipe completed the process; and certainly the labouring-man who emerged less than a minute later was radically different in appearance from the spruce, business-like looking man who had disappeared behind the truck.

Blake strolled up and down the platform, and saw his man leave the train. His actions convinced Blake that he was thoroughly unsuspicious of anything. Alliston hurried away to a cab, and Blake, calling another, followed.

The leading cab twisted in and out through the traffic, and showed from its decisive progress that it had a definite point in view. It eventually pulled up at the docks, and its fare getting out at the head of the wharf, walked quickly towards the other end.

Blake saw there was no time to be lost, and directing his man to drive around the corner into a near-by street, he jumped out and had the cab wait. Strolling back around the corner he leisurely proceeded toward the dock, filling a short, blackened clay pipe as he went along. He looked the every day casual labourer, and his presence on the wharf would excite no suspicion from the already unsuspicious quarry.

As he entered the large shed he quickened his steps, and threaded his way between the bales which half filled it. He went through a large door near the further end, and as he got to the tiny walk which ran around the narrow wharf between the shed and the edge, he saw Alliston standing at the head of a flight of steps watching the approach of a small boat. It was rowed by two sailors, and a man in a captain's uniform sat in the stern. Blake, glancing up, saw a rakish-looking steam-yacht, and could just distinguish the name on her bows—the Mercedes.

When Blake took the case for young Alliston, he had naturally looked up the family history, and his notes showed that the late Charles Alliston had a yacht which had been out of commission since the death of his wife. Her name was the Mercedes, and Blake knew she lay before him.

"He is making hay while the sun shines," muttered the detective to himself. "She looks ready for a cruise, but I'm afraid you are doomed to be disappointed, my friend. Looks as though he was going out to her." Blake was casting around in his mind for some method of following when the boat reached the wharf, and the man in the stern, stepping out, came up the steps.

He greeted Alliston, and as the two men turned to walk up the wharf, Blake slipped inside the door beside which he had been standing and concealed himself behind a near-by bale. As the footsteps approached he heard voices, but only caught a few words of the conversation. It was the captain speaking, and he listened closely as he heard the few words.

"All right, Mr. Alliston, those arrangements are quite satisfactory to me. Bilton Cove on—"

But the voice had died away, and Blake saw it would be futile to follow.

Emerging from his hiding-place he sat upon the bale, and lit his clay pipe. Leaning over against the edge of the door he could just see the two men standing a short distance up the wharf, but there was no possible way of getting closer without attracting their attention. He sat for some minutes smoking and in deep thought until they parted, and the captain came back down the wharf. He glanced sharply at Blake as he passed, but Blake was the lounging casual labourer to perfection, and the seaman, evidently satisfied with his scrutiny, walked on.

After the boat had returned to the yacht Blake got down from his seat and walked leisurely back to his cab. Driving to his hotel he hastened in and changed his disguise back to that of Mr. Gates.

"You're back soon, guv'nor," said Tinker, as Blake came out of his bed-room.

"Yes, and I've changed our plans. We'll go back to Alliston to-night."

"To-night? Has our man gone back?"

"No, I don't imagine he'll return until to-morrow."

"And are you going to leave him here all alone?" asked the boy.

"Yes," smiled Blake. "I'm afraid he'll have to brave the dangers of this great city without our watchful care."

And Tinker, mystified, went to get ready for the return trip.

Blake turned the driving-wheel over to Tinker, and sat immersed in thought, and although the boy was consumed with curiosity, he did not interrupt. They had covered some twenty miles when Blake roused himself and pulled out a road map. He studied it carefully until the increasing darkness made it impossible to see. He thrust it back into his pocket, and signed to Tinker to stop the car in order to light the lamps.

The powerful front lamps of the car lit up the road for a long distance ahead, and, taking the wheel himself, Blake sent the car forward at a fast rate until they reached Farnham. Instead of continuing on he turned and took the road leading to the left.

"Where are we going, guv'nor?" asked Tinker.

"Back to the coast," replied Blake. "I'll tell you why later."

And silence reigned again, broken only by the steady whirr of the engine as the great grey shape raced steadily ahead into the night, answering every delicate touch of the master hand at the wheel.

As the miles flew behind them, and the farmhouse lights grew rarer, Blake increased the speed of the car, until they were tearing along at a terrific pace. One of the great detective's greatest pleasures was in driving the large, delicately-tuned car, and some of his most delicate problems were solved as man and machine bounded over the quiet roads at night while the rest of the world slept. And on this night he needed a clear mind. He was frankly puzzled, and his mind worked mathematically over every point of the problem.

"Curious," he said to himself. "That one point has prevented the joining up of the circle. Everything complete but it. The problem needs that one thing to solve it, but it seems impossible he can have accomplished it. No. The other man must be still—but why the yacht?" And his keen mind went on analysing the problem which was lacking in one essential point.

They had passed through several sleeping villages without a stop, and the salt-laden air told Tinker they were near the coast. The detective brought the car down to a slower pace, and as they reached the brow of a hill he stopped altogether.

Below them lay a small village with an occasional light gleaming forth, and the thatched roofs appearing and disappearing as the light from a revolving lighthouse, on the right, swung round over them. Blake got from the car, and stepping in front of the road light again consulted his map. Apparently satisfied with his inspection he resumed his seat, and, turning the car, started on the return trip.

They arrived at Alliston late, and Tinker slept soundly most of the way, lulled to sleep by the steady murmur of the engine.

Blake gave Tinker some lengthy instructions the next morning, and sent the promised telegram to Inspector Thomas.

THE SEVENTEENTH CHAPTER. The Chase—Blake Again Scores—Alliston Rescued—Harris Captured.

IT was a moonless night. The stars were obscured by heavy clouds, and the darkness was intense. A chill mist-laden breeze gave promise of coming rain, and the rustling of the leaves in the great trees surrounding Alliston Hall gave forth a dreary sound in the darkness. It was a night for the enjoyment of a book before the fire, and the deserted condition of the roads testified to the fact that most of the residents of the village were decidedly of that impression. The few who were abroad were mostly young men on their way to the cosy interior of some cottage where a blushing maiden awaited their coming, and sat nervously fingering her sewing while the clock seemed to drag with unaccustomed slowness.

The bleak night seemed to have its charms for at least one human being, for as the wind got more heavily mist-laden, a dark figure walked cautiously through the impenetrable gloom of the wood surrounding the Hall. He had been standing motionless for some time, evidently watching for some expected occurrence, for as a light shone through a small window at the top of the house and after a few moments, disappearing, near the garage, he smiled grimly, and muttered to himself:

"The impossible has happened. Luck certainly played into your hands, my friend, and you would have stood a good chance of winning out but for those four mistakes you made." And, creeping silently through the trees, Blake—for it was he—moved cautiously over toward the garage.

The light he had seen came from the lamps of a motor-car, and its circle shone on what was evidently of interest to the watching detective, for his eyes never shifted their position.

●   ●   ●   ●   ●

John Alliston hummed to himself as he dressed. Life held an interesting and rosy outlook for him. Things were running on oiled wheels. Business at the mills was good, his income was more than he could spend; Jack, who would be coming home soon for the holidays, had accepted him with out question, the alterations to the Hall were finished, and it only needed a mistress, and the securing of the Honourable Violet Raymonde as that mistress didn't look beyond the realms of possibility. The yacht had been beautifully refitted, and would provide the means for an ideal honeymoon. Only one thing smudged the glass, and that would be wiped away that night. Yes, life certainly looked good to John Alliston.

He was going to the Raymondes' for dinner the next night, and would ask Lord Raymonde for permission to speak to his daughter the following afternoon. Raymonde seemed to like him, and he wasn't a catch to be sniffed at. Certainly the Honourable Vi had seemed a bit offish with him, but she only needed a little delicate handling to capitulate. She would naturally be a bit shy of a man who had married as he had in his younger days; and, by the way, it was about time to get things going. And as he finished dressing, he opened the door and descended to the library.

A man sat in front of the fire, and if Blake had been present, he would have recognised the one to whom Alliston had been speaking on the dock at Liverpool.

"Well, captain, I'm sorry to keep you waiting," remarked Alliston, as he entered.

"Oh, I was comfortable!" replied the other, with a strong nasal twang. "I guess this night ought to about suit our purpose," he added, as the window shook under a blast of wind.

"Yes, fine; it's dark, and going to rain," replied Alliston.

"Well, let's get to business," continued the captain. "It's a long trip, and I want to get started. Have you got the contract ready?"

"Yes; it's all ready for signing, and Harris can witness it. Do you wish to read it?"

"Yes, I reckon I'd better. It's just a regular five year contract," he added, as he passed the paper back.

"Certainly. It gives you a guaranteed berth for five years, and £1,000 cash. Isn't that sufficient?"

"Yes, that's good enough for me. I wouldn't tackle anything so risky as this, but I'm getting along, and, by gosh, I've got a family of girls to keep that don't seem to ever intend getting married."

Alliston laughed as he laid down the paper.

"I'm sorry for that, captain, but this night's work ought to put you on your feet pretty well. I think we'd better finish the other details before Harris comes in. He's all right, but I suppose you prefer this part done without a witness."

"You bet your life I do. This is a serious game to me, and I don't want any third party to see what money I get. He might force me to split some time." And the cautious Yankee skipper smiled.

"I've got the notes all ready for you." And as he spoke, Alliston moved to a small safe, and, opening it, withdrew a package. Tossing it over to the captain, he said, "You'll find them all right, I think; they're in fifties."

The captain picked it up and ran through the notes.

"A thousand," he said, as he finished. "That's right, and thank you, although it's worth more," he added, as he thrust them in his pocket.

"That was your own price." answered Alliston.

"I know; and, by heck, I'll stick to it. And, what's more, you won't find me turning up in the future, like some people, for more. A sure five years' berth and a thousand cash suits Silas Hepner. I ain't no hog."

But the unselfish captain was to be rewarded with a ten years' berth instead of a five years', only his uniform was to be decorated with arrows instead of gold stripes. And, sad to relate, he was not long to retain that attractive package of fifties which rested so snugly inside his coat.

"Well, we'll get Harris in to witness the contract, and then you can be getting along," said Alliston. "I would like to have you remain for dinner, but I'm afraid it would make it too late."

Harris entered a moment later, and the rest of the business being completed, the three cheerful rascals ascended the stairs to the garret.

"Did you give him the draught, Harris?" asked Alliston, as they went up.

"Yes, and he ought to sleep until he gets to Bilton."

"Good! But you'd better keep him well bound, captain, in case he does wake. We can't afford to have a hitch occur."

"You leave it to me," answered the captain. "I contracted to tie a weight to him and drop him in deep water, and, by heck, that's where he's going to be dropped."

"All right! I'll depend on you."

Harris fitted a key in the door of the garret-room, and the light he carried revealed the bound body of a man on the floor, which they proceeded to pick up.

"Gosh! He's heavy!" grunted the captain, as they carried him down.

"He was heavier than that when he came," grinned Harris. "He doesn't seem to have enjoyed the food during his visit."

"Has James got the car ready?" broke in Alliston.

"Yes; he's waiting now," replied Harris.

No other words were spoken until they reached the garage, and, entering the circle of light, formed the scene which proved so interesting to Sexton Blake.

James and the captain entered the car, and James, taking the wheel, they slipped from the garage down the drive, while Alliston and Harris returned to the house.

Alliston sighed with relief as he dined that evening. The last smudge had been wiped from the mirror, and it threw back an undimmed reflection.

.   .   .   .   .

Blake had turned as the car disappeared down the drive, and, making his way through the trees with the certainty and caution of a redskin, he gained the high road and started for the village at a rapid pace.

His thoughts were very busy as he went along. He had put his finger on the explanation he needed for the one missing link, but until his own eyes that night had shown his deductions to be correct, he had deemed it almost impossible. But he had included it in his plans, and had, as was his wont, prepared to meet it. Ever since his return from Liverpool, he had kept unceasing watch on his man; he had hardly eaten, and had not slept at all. Hastening into the inn, he entered the sitting-room where Tinker sat reading.

"Everything is ready, is it?" he asked.

"Yes, guv'nor; I kept things prepared for a quick run, as you told me."

"Very well. Where is Inspector Thomas?"

"In his room, I think."

"Call him, and tell him to put on a warm coat. Get one on yourself also. We've got a long chase ahead of us. Tell the inspector to hurry, or he'll be left behind," he added, as he entered his own room.

Tinker and the inspector will never forget that ride. Blake had put them both in the tonneau, and, sitting at the wheel himself, had taken the road leading through Farnham to Bilton.

Once clear of the village, he had put on speed, and never before had the great grey car thundered at such a pace. He leaned tensely forward, and his keen eyes watched ahead. He knew he would have a fairly clear run, for the roads were deserted. The car seemed to take on part of the man's mentality, for it shot ahead straight and true, answering every touch with an almost reasoning power. Woods, fields, farmyards and villages swept by as they raced madly on, and Tinker and the inspector clinging desperately to the seat, had only a blurred impression of passing objects. Up hills and down hills they tore, over the level, and around sharp turnings, and never once did either machine or driver hesitate.

Miles had whirled by when, as they came to a long level stretch, Blake got a momentary glimpse of a small red light which disappeared almost immediately. The air was heavy with salt, and he knew it had gone over the brow of the hill leading down to Bilton. It would be touch and go, and instead of slackening speed as he reached the brow of the hill, he kept on, and the machine tore down at a terrific pace, almost causing the sudden death of the inspector from heart-faint.

Blake eased up a bit as they came to the village street, and as he turned the corner and took the road leading to the beach, he again saw the small red light ahead of him. As everything was lit up by the rays of the revolving lighthouse, he saw it was the car he was after. Out in the harbour could be seen the lights of a ship, and he put it on faster, knowing he was on the right trail.

The driver of the other car had seen them, for Blake was not gaining, and their quarry must have put on full speed to keep the lead. As they tore on, the pursuers saw a lantern lifted from the car ahead. It was waved in a circle, and an answering signal came from the ship in the bay.

The front car reached the shore and stopped at the edge of the water, lifting out their burden. And as they did so, Blake dashed up and stopped his car, with the front wheels in the water.

As they jumped out and rushed towards the other, they heard the sound of oars, and realised their work must be quickly done.

The body was lying on the ground, and Blake could make out James and the captain beside it. As he and his companions rushed up, the other two fired, but their aim was wild in the dark. The sound of oars was growing nearer, and the captain called to his men to hurry, but they still had some hundred yards to cover.

Hardly had he done so when Blake, Tinker, and the inspector

closed in. The struggle was short and sharp, but they soon had the bracelets on the pair, and hustling them over, they tossed them over into the tonneau of Blake's car. Picking up the other body, they placed it in the car belonging to the prisoners.

"Take the inspector and drive my car," called Blake to Tinker. "I'll follow with the other."

Tinker backed the big car out of the water, and turned, heading up the beach; and as Blake followed, the boat reached the shore, but the cars had gathered speed and left them behind.

They pulled up on top of the big hill and unbound the man in the car Blake was driving. He was still asleep, so they laid him back in the seat to come round.

"By George, that was hot!" gasped the inspector, as they walked over to look at their captives. "I don't understand who they are or what your plan is!" he grumbled.

"You won't, either," smiled Blake. "I told you. I would turn over the Alliston murderer to you. Well, he's nowhere. But these two are accomplices of his, and if you don't get impatient you will be credited with the biggest haul for years."

"Well, you might give me some light on the matter," said the inspector, but his old habit reasserted itself, and he visibly swelled when Blake spoke of the "biggest haul."

Blake could not resist just that little revenge, and refused to enlighten the inspector further.

"We'll go on to Liverpool and put these two under lock and key," he said. "To-morrow we will go back to Alliston, and I'll keep my promise to you, inspector."

"Who is the man we released?" asked the inspector.

"Well," replied Blake, "I think, when he comes round, he will give his name as John Alliston," and, disregarding the inspector's puzzled look and Tinker's delighted grin, he climbed into the captured car and led the way towards Liverpool.

John Alliston was better the next morning, and on their way back to Alliston village, he told Blake the details of his capture.

"But aren't you afraid the mate of the yacht will send a warning?" he asked as he finished.

"No," replied Blake; "he is probably the only one on the yacht who is in on the thing with the captain, and he will be too careful of his own skin. He won't know anything positive as we got away so quickly, and he will wait for further information before he does anything."

They arrived at Alliston village early in the evening, and proceeded straight to the Hall.

Blake rang the bell, and as the four waited he put Alliston out of sight behind him.

Harris answered the ring, and recognised Blake, but couldn't distinguish the faces of the others.

"Is Mr. Alliston at home?" inquired Blake.

"No, sir; he has gone to Lord Raymonde's for dinner. Did you come to see him about the case, sir?"

"Yes," replied Blake; "and I will see him without fail later in the evening. But I think you are mistaken, Harris, when you say Mr. Alliston is not at home," and as he spoke he thrust John Alliston forward into the light.

Harris gave a gasp, and his nerve went to pieces, for he saw the game was up. They bound him and locked him in the garret-room for the night and then headed the car for Lord Raymonde's.

THE EIGHTEENTH CHAPTER.   Blake Keeps His Word to the Inspector—The End of theTrail—Blake Explains.

THE pseudo John Alliston timed his leaving the Hall in order to arrive at Lord Raymonde's a half-hour before dinner. He considered everything was now on a sound basis for the future, and that he could risk asking the Honourable Vi to become his wife; and, indeed, Fate seemed to be working with him, for, on his arrival, he found Lord Raymonde in the library alone. He had a houseful of guests—he always had—but they were evidently all in their rooms, dressing.

"Ah, Alliston!" said Lord Raymonde, as he was ushered in. "You're early, but glad you are. I'm done a bit early myself to-night, and we can have a chat before the other's come. Pull up a chair and have a cigarette. Beastly weather! Been a steady spell of it now. Sad thing that aeroplane accident at the manoeuvres!" And he rattled on in his cheery way while Alliston seated himself and lit a cigarette.

"To tell you the truth, Lord Raymonde, I came early for a particular purpose to-night. I—or—I realise I made a beastly mistake in my younger days; but that was some years ago now, and I—well, to put it bluntly, Lord Raymonde—I want your permission to ask the Honourable Violet to become my wife— Wait, hear me out, please," he added, as Lord Raymonde started to speak. "I realise that the last ten years of my life is unknown to you, but I can assure you my record is clean during that period. I deeply admire your daughter, and if she consents to become my wife I think I could make her happy. You know," he added, laughing apologetically, "I'm not a pauper."

"Well, Alliston, I must confess this is a great surprise to me. I never dreamed you admired Vi in that way. But still, if you care for her and she reciprocates your affections, why, I have no objections. By the way, she's not at home to-night. She went over to the Hungerford's to dinner."

"Thank you—thank you, Lord Raymonde. I will try my fate with her to-morrow."

"Very well, Alliston. Good luck to you! Ah, Sir Walter! Come in! We all seem to be getting around early tonight," he added, as Sir Walter Hall entered, and the conversation shifted to general topics.

Dinner was announced shortly after, and they filed in. Lord Raymonde was a widower, and the guests were all men, so the Honourable Vi's absence caused a lack of any feminine element at the table. Most of the guests were intimates of the host, and among them were Sir Walter Hall and Doctor Thornton, who had been there at the time of Blake's previous visit. Several other congenial spirits made up the party, and after Alliston had been introduced all round, conversation started, and before very long Sir Walter Hall was riding his hobby of "crime and the criminal." Most of the others had heard it often, but Alliston, being a stranger, and, although the others did not know it, very interested in the subject, listened attentively as Sir Walter warmed to his subject.

"As I told Sexton Blake," he was saying, "I think, if a criminal is really clever and makes his crime a profession, he can operate without fear of discovery."

"I agree with you, Sir Walter," replied Alliston. "In my opinion, if a man keeps up with science he can plan and commit a crime without any fear of detection."

"I still hold a contrary opinion," came a cold, icy voice from the doorway, and, looking up, they saw Sexton Blake standing there.

His eyes rested steadily on Alliston as he spoke, who showed in that moment the secret of his past daring successes, for he hesitated for only the fraction of a second. He slipped his hand into the pocket of his waistcoat, and withdrawing it, brushed it carelessly across his mouth and continued speaking, as though nothing had happened. Yet, in that quiet voice from the door sounded the death-knell of all his hopes and plans.

"Of course, I am always open to conviction," he said, "and in this case, gentlemen, I have been convinced. I withdraw the opinion I expressed. I agree with Mr. Blake thoroughly, gentlemen. I beg your pardon, Lord Raymonde, for—"

But he had crashed forward on the table, the poison capsule having quickly done its deadly work.

Blake leaped for him as he fell, and the others jumped up from the table; but life was already extinct. He was a clever criminal, and probably Sexton Blake best summed him up:

"Gentlemen, there died a man who had the makings in him of one of the greatest specialists in crime."

He turned the body over to Inspector Thomas, who departed with it, Tinker driving him to the hotel. Blake brought Alliston in, and Lord Raymonde insisted on extra covers being laid. Everyone was naturally upset by the tragedy, but those who had lost their appetites over the affair stuck it out in hopes that the great detective would enlighten them, and they were not disappointed.

When the servants had left and cigars had been lighted, Blake, at Lord Raymonde's earnest request, consented to explain the details of his deductions which led to the running to earth of Saunders.

•　　•　　•　　•　　•

"When I went over to Alliston Hall," began Blake, "I had no intention of taking up the case, and only looked around casually before Inspector Thomas arrived. The case naturally interested me from a professional point of view; but I was busy at the time, and would not have gone ahead on its investigation if the murdered man's grandson, Jack, hadn't begged me to do so. He was alone in the world, and my cursory examination had convinced me of a master brain behind the deed. Consequently, in view of the circumstances, and for the boy's protection, I took it on.

"Inspector Thomas formed a theory that it had been committed by someone coming to the window and calling Mr. Alliston out, and murdering him under the trees. I formed a different theory, for the perpetrator had made four mistakes," and he smiled at Sir Walter. "The murder was committed inside the house, and I will tell you how I know:

"Firstly.—As you remember reading in the papers at the time, there were two lots of footprints—one leading up to the window and returning from it, supposed to be the murderer's; and one leading away from the window, but not returning, supposed to be Mr. Alliston's. Gentlemen, the footprints of the murderer started from the window and returned to it, showing they originated from the library, for where they came into contact with each other the footprints leading to the window overlapped those leading from the window."

Dead silence reigned at the table as Blake sipped his coffee and continued:

"Secondly.—Both pairs of footprints measured in every particular exactly the same, showing they were made from the same last, and belonged to one person. The shoes on Mr. Alliston's feet, gentlemen, were of those same measurements proving an extra pair of his shoes had been used for the deception."

"By Jove! Who would have thought it!" murmured Sir Walter.

"Thirdly," continued Blake—"The single line of footprints were deeper than even a very heavy man would make in the mud—they were nearly twice as deep as the others — and we know Mr. Alliston was not heavy. And, besides, the irregular impression showed that the man who made them carried a heavy burden, which it was safe to assume was the body, for that line of footprints stopped where the body was found.

"Fourthly.—At the place where the body was left was the impression of a left hand with the little finger missing, and also the mark left by a person who had sat down, showing that the man who had carried the body had seated himself on the grass for some purpose. Working on the theory of the shoes, it showed me that he had done so in order to put on his own shoes, after taking off Mr. Alliston's, which he had been wearing, to replace them on the murdered man's feet. As he put his hand down to assist him to his feet, it left the imprint in the mud as the weight of the body came on it.

"Those things proved to me that the crime had been committed in the house, and at the examination by Inspector Thomas, when Harris, the butler, obliterated the finger-marks by stepping on them, I knew that he had been concerned in the crime, because he made a longer step than was natural with him in order to put his on it, and turned round unnecessarily, to be sure he had obliterated it.

"When Jack asked me to take the case and I consented, I naturally looked up the family history, and Jack himself told me his father had the little finger of his left hand missing. That, at first, placed Mr. Alliston in my mind as the perpetrator of the deed"—and he smiled at Mr. Alliston— "but further inquiry showed me Harris had only been there a short time, and exhaustive investigation in London proved his criminal record. Consequently, the murderer must have been John Alliston, or someone impersonating him, to lay such elaborate plans. If it was an impersonation, it wasn't natural that the impersonator would have his little finger missing before he laid his plans. Therefore he must have got it done for the purpose. A thorough canvass of the London doctors gained the information that a man with an uninjured hand had had the little finger of the left hand amputated, and had been very particular to have it taken off exactly as he directed. That showed a knowledge of the real John Alliston.

"When the murderer fled in the motor-car I picked up his trail, and inquiry by Tinker, my assistant, disclosed the fact that a passenger had just gained the Caronia, on the morning following the murder, before she sailed for New York. I immediately sent him to New York on the Mauretania, and she docked before the Caronia."

A murmur of admiration ran round the table as Blake stopped to puff his cigar. Continuing, he said:

"Tinker, unfortunately, was 'shanghaied' by the rascals agents in New York, and I went over to find him. I won't go into the details of those weeks, but it is sufficient to say that I eventually located him on board a steamer going to the Arctic, from which I succeeded in rescuing him.

"My trip to New York was fortunate, for I got track there of the real John Alliston, and found he had gone to Nevada. The police in Reno Nevada discovered that a man sentenced for life, under the name of William Torrence, had confided, to his lawyer before he went to prison that his name was John Alliston. I traced him to the prison, but the authorities wrote me that William Torrence, or convict No. 8072, had been pardoned after ten years for saving many lives during the prison fire. There I lost him, but he was an element that must be found.

"A man had returned and taken the position and name of John Alliston while I was in New York. My investigations in Nevada showed that there was some doubt of the guilt of William Torrence, and the fact was brought to light that shortly after his sentence a man named James Carson, who had been in the Red Dog saloon, apparently drunk, the night of the murder for which Torrence was committed, had left there a few months after with plenty of money. I had to put a lot of machinery in motion, but I eventually traced him to London, where he had been operating on the Exchange under the name of James Ford. He went broke on rubber, and disappeared, turning up later as William Saunders. I now knew that he might be impersonating John Alliston, but I could not proceed against him until I had the real one.

"The impersonator coolly wrote me, asking me to run down and discuss the case with him, but I sent a reply which allayed any suspicions he may have had of me.

"The confidence of his actions showed me he must feel sure of himself, and the mathematical proof of my deductions made it certain he must feel pretty safe about the real John Alliston. I considered the possibility of his having been able to get hold of the real one, but it was almost impossible that luck would so play into his hands; but later events proved my reasoning to be correct, and Mr. Alliston afterwards told me how it happened." And Blake went on to relate how Alliston had been captured.

"I knew when I had written my letter to him that if he had Alliston, or could place his hand on him, he would act soon to clear everything away for the future, and I watched him every minute. He fulfilled my expectations to the letter, and you saw the result to-night."

The silence remained unbroken for some moments after the great detective finished speaking. Finally, Sir Walter Hall spoke.

"By Jove! Mr. Blake, you astound me! Yes, sir, I say it—you astound me! Why, sir, you have changed my opinions which I have held for years!" And the others smiled at the shaking-up which Sir Walter's hobby had received.

"You are not the only one who changed their opinion on that subject to-night, Sir Walter," answered Blake quietly.

Discussion on the case became general around the table, and such is human nature, that the interest of the detective's narrative drove from their minds the depression caused by the tragedy earlier in the evening.

Lord Raymonde was silent, thinking of the conversation he had had in the library before dinner, but wisely decided not to mention it. He was thankful for his escape, and shuddered to think what it would have meant if the Honourable Vi had accepted the pseudo John Alliston and the exposure had come then.

    •   •   •   •   •

Crowestoft School once more had Sexton Blake for a visitor, but this time John Alliston accompanied him. The doctor soon came to greet them, and a few words explained to that astonished gentleman the true state of affairs.

He took Alliston along with him until Blake had broken the news to Jack, then father and son would meet. Jack soon came and shook hands warmly with the great detective.

"Did father send you to me about the murder case, Mr. Blake?"

"Er—hardly, Jack. I'm afraid, my boy, you must make up your mind for a bit of a shock," replied Blake.

"What is it, Mr. Blake?" cried the boy. "Is it bad news?"

"It's a long story, Jack, and I'll try to tell it quickly. Just listen carefully." And Blake gently told him of Saunders' impersonation and his real father's return.

"But, sir," said Jack, almost piteously, as Blake finished, "I can hardly credit it. He didn't seem a bit like a criminal. It seems awful that I accepted grandfather's murderer as my father. Is my father—my real father—coming to see me, sir?"

"He's here now, Jack," smiled Blake. "I'll bring him. Just wait here."

A moment later Blake returned with Alliston. He turned away as father and son met, but not before he had seen in Jack's eyes that the real father was all that the boy could wish. His heart would hunger no longer for a father's love.

He slipped quietly away as father and son sat down, oblivious of everything, and left them alone for half an hour.

The doctor returned with him, and Blake made preparations to leave, as he had to get back to town.

He said good-bye to Jack, and turned to Alliston. He was surprised to see tears in the big man's eyes, but John Alliston was greatly shaken with emotion.

"Good-bye, Mr. Blake!" he said huskily, gripping Blake's hand. "You've given me more happiness than I ever dreamed of. Little did I think, when I lay surrounded by the grim prison walls, that I would ever see home again and have my boy. I owe it all to you."

The doctor accompanied the busy detective to the door, and a little later he dropped into his easy-chair in Baker Street with a tired sigh.

"Well, I've got no son," he mused, "but I don't know that I wouldn't as soon have Tinker and Pedro!"

    •   •   •   •   •

Six months later the real John Alliston had an interview in the library with Lord Raymonde, which was very similar to that of his late impersonator. But Fate dealt more kindly with him, and he led the radiantly beautiful Honourable Vi to the altar shortly after. Sexton Blake was best man, and Tinker and Pedro were very much in evidence.

THE END.

[36600 WORDS]

Other content, not available include: A Word From the Skipper (ed.); Charlie Gordon's Schooldays by Henry St. John, serial.

www.ingramcontent.com/pod-product-compliance
Lightning Source LLC
Chambersburg PA
CBHW031851170626
46807CB00004B/1668